AN EROTIC ROMANCE

JUST ONE
Night
VOL. 1-3

I0451632

Completed Story

KIM BLACK

Just One Night by Kim Black

Volume I-III

Editing by
Nicki Kuzn & Donna Bayar Repsher

Kim Black Books
ISBN-13: 978-0996381017
ISBN-10: 0996381015

ABOUT THE AUTHOR

International Amazon Bestselling Author Kim Black is a born and raised New Yorker. She is engaged to a wonderful man and loves spending time at home with her family. She currently resides in Bronx, NY, but is a true Brooklyn girl. You can take the girl out of Brooklyn…

From the time Kim picked up her first book at her middle school library, she fell in love with the feeling of getting lost in another world. Books became her escape and she dove head first into the many books she loved with joy. She strives to provide that same feeling for her readers.

In 2011, she was introduced to the world of erotic romance and fell in love with the genre, reading any and everything she could get her hands on. By the following year, she decided to take a chance at self-publishing an erotic romance series and thankfully she has been fortunate enough to have gained a fan base, though she still finds it unbelievable.

While Kim Black may be known for her angst and suspenseful, sexy romances, she is working on branching out into other romance genres.

Kim holds a Degree in Graphic Design and Animation and is the CEO of a new publishing services company, TOJ Publishing Services, where she provides authors with custom graphics, marketing and promotional services.

She is also a proud PRO member of Romance Writers of America and is a part of two of their chapters: RWA-NYC and KOD-RWA. ♥

BOOK DESCRIPTION

One night is all Blake Hanson requires.
Tomorrow he will move on to
the next eager and willing sub.
And women are always eager for him.
No commitments. No feelings.
Just Sex.
It is his only rule. His guide.
And he never loses control, until...

~~~~

The night isn't over for Blake Hanson
Not by a long shot
He needs more, craved it even
A round two, so to speak.
He knows that Alyson Lane is trouble
Trouble that he should avoid at all cost
Still, he can't keep away
And neither can she...

~~~~

Alyson Lane thinks that she can leave,
but she will not walk away from this.
From Me.
Alyson hasn't realized it yet,
but she's made a big mistake.
It's one thing to agree to go our separate ways,
it's another to shoot Blake Hanson down.
No, Alyson chose wrong and
I am going to make sure she knows it.
I am not a man to be turned away from.
I will not be denied.
She is my sub and I...

AN EROTIC ROMANCE

JUST ONE
Night

VOL. 1

BLAKE

I don't do relationships, ever! I have no use for them. All I want I can find in the encounters I arrange online. One night with a beautiful sub, willing to allow me to do whatever I desire to her. Total control.

There are no questions, no dinners and no awkward unnecessary conversations. There's just me, my sub and the private suite at The Dungeon.

Why? Because I can. I can do without the necessary obligations that come with relationships. There's no need for me to expose my personal, private inner demons or to offer up some weak part of myself only to have the relationship shatter to pieces in the end.

I have no time for that shit!

At least I'm not a dick about it. I always lay my cards on the table the second they answer my ad. I'm never one to mislead them into my bed—I don't have to. One look at my picture, the same picture I've been using for the past three years, and they agree to my terms. It's worked every single time.

The woman with me tonight is no exception. She hadn't waited even ten minutes before she was begging to meet me, promising that I would never regret meeting her.

So far… she's okay. She's nothing special, there's nothing extraordinary about her that might cause me to look at her twice. Her breasts, thighs and pussy are the same as the other countless women I've met and brought into my private suite.

Eagerly looking up at me, she waits for me to instruct her as she kneels before me. She's cute enough, but she's definitely not a knockout. It doesn't matter to me, I won't see her again after tonight.

"I seem to recall instructing you to be ready at 8:00 p.m. sharp," I begin, as I circle the slender, pale-skinned brunette. Her name escapes me, but I remember all that I need to for tonight: her safe word—David, the name of her *dog*.

"Sir, I apologize. I was let out of work late," she offers, her head bowed down to her chest. Her breathing accelerates and I can see that she's already enjoying our little scene.

Stopping behind her, I tug at her hair—not enough to hurt her, just enough to make her gasp in surprise. She looks up at me, her eyes burning with lust.

"You do understand the position you put me in, don't you?" I hiss into her ear, allowing my breath to tease her lobe and cause her to whimper softly.

"Yes, Sir. I… I should be punished," she says, simply.

Releasing her hair, I stroll over to the chest I keep one side of the room, my back turning away from her, where she waits, kneeling. "Kneel, bend over, facing the bed. Panties off. Ass up. Face touching the mattress. And don't move."

I take my time rolling up my sleeves while she makes quick work of removing her panties and positioning herself as instructed. She's eager and I can already smell her arousal.

Opening the chest, I pull out my flogger, a personal favorite of mine. Strutting back over to her where she waits by the bed, I look at her pale ass and lick my lips, anxious to paint her bottom a pretty shade of pink for defying me.

"Hands above your head," I whisper, as I gently caress her skin, noticing her sharp intake of breath at my touch.

She isn't half bad. So eager and so willing. Just the way I like it.

"You like that," I murmur, as I nudge her legs apart.

"Yes, Sir, I do."

Running my right hand over her ass, I grip her meaty flesh before trailing my hand lower.

"Fuck. You're already dripping," I murmur before stepping away from her.

She does as she is told, bringing her hands up high above her head and pushing her bottom up toward me, silently asking me to begin her punishment.

"Only for you, sir."

For tonight, maybe.

ALYSON

What the hell am I doing? I ask myself, as the car I am riding in makes its way along the busy Manhattan streets. My heart is beating a mile a minute with each passing street light.

The seriousness of my agreeing to meet this stranger tonight suddenly weighs heavily on me, and I fight against the growing urge to jump out of the town car he sent over to pick me up.

He hadn't even offered to get me himself; instead, he told me that his car would collect me at 8:00 p.m. sharp. I thought it was rude, but I didn't realize quite how much it would bother me until, well after the car took off, taking me to God knows where.

I hate this feeling in the pit of my stomach, a nagging discomfort that hasn't let up, no matter how much I try to calm my shaky nerves.

He could be a killer. My mind races, thinking of all the possibilities I could be walking into. A killer who is first going to have his way with me, and then dump my body into the Hudson River.

A chill runs through me as I realize that there is a good chance my body won't ever be found should this encounter go south. No one will look for me, since I have no family left to worry about or miss me and no friends to wonder where I've gone. I am completely alone and totally vulnerable to him, to Blake.

Clutching my purse against my chest, I berate myself for telling him that I have no family in the city. I should never have told him that I'm the only survivor of a tragic accident that occurred years ago, a terrible memory that I rarely allow myself to think about, much less speak about. I tucked that memory away fifteen years ago.

He didn't need to know that piece of information, and truthfully, I only told him about it because our email conversations up to that point were all of a sexual nature, never about anything real. I thought that revealing such a personal detail about myself might cause him to divulge something personal about himself in exchange for my admission.

He hadn't.

I have only known the man via email for a week, and now I am on my way to meet him for the first time. I don't know why I had agreed to this date or why I continued talking to him after our online misunderstanding, yet here I am, heading straight into the unknown.

You agreed because you are 22 years old, all alone, and you have never had an orgasm. My inner voice makes me feel pathetic, as I think back to our very first conversation.

I had been surfing the net in search of a job, when I stumbled across an ad which I believed to be for a position as a substitute teacher.

Perfect, I'd thought to myself, as I clicked on the title and began to thoroughly read the ad:

New Sub Needed

Must be clean, in your 20's and experienced. No novices. Headshot required. Contract mandatory.

I was completely confused by the ad. Why would a headshot be required? Why was there no mention of a resume, and why did the school feel it necessary to require that the substitute be clean? *Had they recently employed a bum or something?*

I didn't understand and I wrinkled my nose as I attached both a copy of my resume and a full-body photo of myself. I didn't have professionally taken headshots to send, and I decided that it shouldn't matter what type of photograph I sent. My resume, which highlighted my years of experience as a teaching assistant, from the time I was in high school until the time I graduated college a few months ago, should speak for itself. This job was perfect for me, I thought, as I hit the send button with enthusiasm at the prospect of finding a job after months of searching.

It wasn't until I received a response a few moments later that I realized the error I'd made and it wasn't just a regular mistake, it was a monstrous one, and I was completely mortified as I read the responding email several times.

I see that you aren't capable of following instructions, Ms. Lane. This does not bode well for you if you wish to be my sub. Nonetheless, please answer the following questions to the best of your ability.

The questions that followed had me wide-eyed and confused. They included terms like 'edge play,' 'forced orgasm' and 'rope bondage,' all of which made my cheeks blush red. I immediately Googled each term, eager to understand what this man was referring to. I couldn't help but blush further as I read the definitions.

Do people really do this shit?

A bit curious, I answered each question using my trusty friend, Google, as my guide. I lied my way through each question, thinking there wasn't harm in doing so, but when he sent me an invitation for tonight along with a very improper photo of himself, something told me to say "yes". At the time, that something had been a throbbing ache for the man in the picture, an ache for him to make me feel things I had never felt before. I had no doubt that he would do so, and the eager part of me, already drenched, needed to experience a night with him. This is why I now find myself in this predicament; on my way to meet this bondage sex-god and terrified beyond words, yet still horny as hell for him.

I can only hope that he will send me back home once he discovers that I am unskilled in the art of BDSM. Surely, he won't be too upset with me. It is, after all, just a misunderstanding.

After sending my acceptance to him last night, and using his picture to alleviate the pressure between my legs, I stayed up late researching BDSM, wanting to be prepared for whatever this date might lead to. I know he expects sex; it's a given since that was his purpose in placing the ad in the first place. *I wonder how long he's had it posted. How many women have already responded to him?*

The car slows to a stop at a red light, the busy sounds of the city slightly muffled by the windows suddenly closing, as though the driver knows just what I'm thinking. I can't help but eye the door handle to my left, wondering how crazy it would seem if I suddenly bolted from the town car and ran like mad.

It's not like I'd get very far anyway, I decide, shaking the crazy thought from my head. I'm wearing a form-fitting red lace dress and matching six-inch heels. The driver, who hasn't uttered a single word from the time I climbed in, is fit. Really fit. He'd more than likely catch me before I even rounded the back of the long, black town car.

Rolling my eyes, I decide in that moment that I don't like him, figuring he can't possibly be a good person if he's going to help his employer kill me by driving me to…

Shit, where are we? I wonder, confused, when we veer off a bridge.

Brooklyn?

We're in Brooklyn, I realize, as I read a green sign with white lettering welcoming us into the borough as we weave around several cars.

Sighing, I sink further into the comfortable black leather seat and close my eyes. I know there isn't much I can do to stop this from happening, so I opt to simply accept it for now, figuring that I will just deal with the consequences of my irresponsible choice to meet him once we arrive at our destination.

When the car comes to a stop, I suddenly stiffen up, as I wait for the driver to open my door. I have never been to Brooklyn before, so I don't even bother looking out the window to figure out where he's taken me.

My breathing quickly accelerates as I sit in the back seat, my chest suddenly feeling heavy as I recall the contents of his last email to me this afternoon.

Red dress, high heels, no panties!

See you tonight,

Blake

At the time, I found his message sexy and mysterious, but now, as I sit in the back of his town car in Brooklyn, I don't find it sexy at all.

Instead, I find it both daunting and embarrassing to sit here with my lady parts exposed.

The car door opens and a gust of autumn wind rushes into the car, as the veiny, thick hand of the driver stretches out towards me. I don't make a move to grasp it yet. Instead, I send up a silent prayer to the universe, hoping that something or someone up there will watch over me as I walk into the unknown.

Finally taking his hand, I shimmy out of the town car, careful not to flash the man as I exit. I stand at his side as he closes the door. Once closed, he turns to face me. He is a handsome man, older, but built like a house—a strong man with kind eyes, but I'm not a fool. He looks as though he might be lethal.

He gestures for me to walk ahead of him, his right hand coming to rest at the small of my back. There's an unmarked and dingy building ahead of us, with not a single window at the ground level, a fact which causes my anxiety to spike higher with each step I take.

The sound of my heart thumping in my ears drowns out the clicking of my heels on the pavement along deserted street. All I can do is stare at the rusted metal door ahead of me, wondering what I will find on the other side.

Gulping, I stop in front of the intimidating building and close my eyes tightly, while taking a deep breath meant to still my rising anxiety.

"Right this way, Ms. Lane," I hear a man's voice say, causing me to open my eyes. The driver has the door open and is waiting for me to step through it, a knowing glint now evident in his gaze. He smiles and nods his head and I reluctantly return the gesture.

Maybe he isn't a bad man after all, I consider.

Taking in one last deep breath, I take the first step.

Here goes nothing.

BLAKE

I toss back a shot of brandy and ask for another one before swiveling around in my stool to examine the room. I haven't liked the way I'm feeling since the moment I entered The Dungeon, and I curse myself for asking Alyson to meet me here tonight.

I'm anxious, which doesn't make any sense to me since she is no different than any of the other women I have brought here. Aside from the fact that she has virtually no experience, she is just another beautiful woman. Still, I am nervous.

"Fuck!" I groan, as I look at my watch for the sixth time tonight. They aren't late yet, but I still fight the urge to text Jaxon, my driver and personal assistant, for their ETA.

I need to calm the fuck down. I give the room a once over. One look at the dimly lit club reassures my reasoning for placing the ads. The women here are boring, offering me no challenge, and I've already run through most of the regulars. I'm not one to linger with a sub past the contract's expiration date.

One night.

It's all I require, all I need, after which I will move on to the next sub. I know most men don't bother with contracts for a single night, but being a successful corporate lawyer as well as a silent partner in The Dungeon, I know the importance of covering my ass. I always have the women sign a contract the second they set foot in my suite. I won't chance a woman crying abuse in the hopes of bleeding me dry should she recognize me in the papers.

It's never happened, still I always insist on their signatures, ensuring that both me and my multi-million dollar portfolio are safe.

I'm not sure why I even entertained Alyson's response to my ad. It was obvious to me that she lied about her previous experience as soon as I read her textbook, generic responses. I surmised that she got her answers from either the internet or from erotic novels. I don't want a sub who requires training, which is why I always specify "experience required" in my ads. Training takes both time and patience—neither of which I possess.

I'm not a man who is eager to show off his prowess as a Master. I have no interest in finding an apprentice to teach how to submit. These things require too much of me. I'm not the kind of man to take lightly the responsibility of jumping into such a delicate situation, knowing that choosing a trainee requires careful thought and consideration. Personalities and expectations are a major factor in selecting and training a sub. I know this all too well, given the manner in which I was first introduced to this lifestyle.

When Alyson wrote that her hard limits where that she wasn't as physically flexible as she would like to be, I nearly choked on my drink, laughing hysterically. It's a uncommon thing for me to do, but at the time, I couldn't help but chuckle as I continued reading.

Curious to see what she Googled, I searched for the words 'hard limits' and 'flexible' and nearly died laughing at what I found:

HARD LIMIT: A limit which is considered to be absolute, inflexible, and non-negotiable.

Assuming she read the same definition, she obviously focused her attention on the inflexible part and missed the meaning altogether. I couldn't help but chuckle at her apparent naiveté.

Although I was amused by her complete lack of experience, I had every intention of deleting her email and continuing my search. I have a strict 'no novice' policy when I select a sub. One night encounters aren't really ideal for training subs, but the picture she sent along with her initial resume stopped me from doing so.

The photo showed a stunningly breathtaking woman with curves I wanted to feel under my hands, and long, toned legs I eagerly desired to feel wrapped around my waist. Intrigued by the look of her, rather than hitting the delete button, I found myself clicking 'reply' and it went downhill from there.

Fifteen.

That was the number of emails that were exchanged between us since the first, and it makes me groan with irritation just thinking about it. Although, I must admit, I did enjoy it. I'm not normally the type to sit and chit-chat with women online. I'm sure as hell not one to tolerate a woman's charade either, and yet I did, which is why I'm upset as I sit here at the bar inside this exclusive club, waiting for her to arrive.

What irritates me most is that I'm not sure with whom I am more upset, myself, for engaging her or her, for lying to me.

Turning back to the bar, I pick up the glass of brandy the bartender has refilled and down it, wincing slightly, as the liquid burns its way down my throat. I'm not much of a drinker, preferring to always stay in control, but the few of my rules I've already broken with this woman, has me needing something to take the edge off.

"Thanks," I mutter to the young bartender, dressed in only his FemDomme's collar and dark colored jeans.

Standing up, I make my way through the dark club, carefully studying each exhibit. Each scene is showcased with a different soft colored spotlight, and features either another couple or a group. Some couples are completely engrossed in one another, using whips and/or chains, while others only tease their partners with hooded, lustful stares, and/or soft, alluring touches.

The ground floor of the club is considered the area for 'Basic' play. Nothing remarkable goes on down here, it's primarily the place for foreplay and fetish fantasies. The top two floors, known as 'Elite', are where the real action takes place, but not all members are granted access to those floors, certainly not without first being restricted to the ground floor for a time.

The Dungeon prides itself on exclusivity and discretion, and only after a thorough background and financial check are members allowed to explore what the 'Elite' has to offer. Being an owner, I have my pick of any room or floor in the establishment.

"Mr. Hanson."

I turn to look behind me at the sound of my name and spot my driver making his way toward me, with Alyson shyly trailing along behind him. Her long legs are the first thing I notice, and I can't help but drink her in as more of her comes into view.

Fucking stunning. This is going to be interesting.

ALYSON

The lobby tells me absolutely nothing about this place. It is a bare, all white room containing only an elevator.

Allowing the driver to escort me inside, I continue to take calming breaths as we begin to ascend. I glance at the driver who stands next to me, contemplating whether or not I should ask him about this place. He seems to be somewhat approachable, but I can't really be certain of that, so I keep my mouth shut and my questions to myself.

The elevator soon dings, signaling that we have reached our floor. Stepping out first, I feel the hand of the driver return to the small of my back. I don't know why, but I suddenly feel safe with his hand there. Perhaps it's because of the small smile he gave me downstairs.

"You have nothing to worry about Ms. Lane," he says suddenly, without turning to look at me.

Stopping dead in my tracks, I turn to look him in the face.

"What makes you think I'm worried," I ask, not liking the fact that my emotions were apparently so easy for him to read.

He shrugs, "I meant no offense. I apologize," he whispers, with a knowing glint in his eyes.

I don't like that glint or the fact that he seems to be having a great time watching me panic.

Was this the way it had been with all the other women Blake had picked up online?

Turning away from him, I notice that the long hallway in which we are now standing has only one door at the very end. I begin making my way toward it, while the driver remains close by my side.

"Just tell…" I begin to blurt out, but my voice trails off as we reach the door. I gather my thoughts and try again, "I'm not walking in there to meet a rapist or murderer, am I?"

I don't look up at him as I ask, not sure whether or not I really want to hear his response. I hate that I appear to be so weak and uncertain in front of him, but I just can't walk through that door without asking, without getting some kind of reassurance.

The driver chuckles softly, forcing me to look at him with some annoyance. "That is not funny!" I fume, with my hands at my hips.

Reining in his laughter, the driver straightens up, and replies, "I'm sorry. It's just… I already like you. I hope he keeps you around."

Not giving me a chance to respond, the driver opens the wooden door, and a cacophony of sound assaults my ears. I can hear the faint sounds of music, but there is something else overlaying the melody. I gasp, and bring my hands up to my mouth as I take in the room, realization hitting me strongly.

Holy shit!

I know as soon as we step inside the room that Blake has brought me to a sex club, and I shudder with nervousness as the sounds coming from the room grow even louder as the driver leads me inside.

Fuck, fuck, fuck. What the hell am I doing here?

I not ready to explore this place, unsure of what I will find once we are fully inside, but the driver stops my forward movement and asks me to hold on for a minute.

Thankful for a moment to think, I contemplate turning away and leaving. I am not ready for this.

No one man is worth all this shit. A sex club? What the hell is this man into?

Sure, the idea of meeting him, and of possibly experiencing my first real orgasm was enticing before, but now that I'm here, I'm not sure I can go through with it as panic starts to envelop me. My hands are suddenly clammy and my heart is racing

Looking over at the driver, I see that he is speaking to someone who appears to be a hostess, dressed in what can only be referred to as underwear. I can't hear what they are saying, but I notice that he and the woman exchange cards, or at least that's what it looks like from where I'm standing.

A few seconds later he returns to me with a smile on his face, "Right this way…"

The décor is flawless. Luxurious draperies line the club's walls; they are all white and each exhibit is backlit. I take it all in with wide, astonished eyes, as we make our way through the club.

The solid, stark white, Greek columns make the place appear regal. Soft, majestic music plays in the background amid the human grunts, moans and yelps, causing me to instinctively hide shyly behind the driver. I know that I am in way over my head, but I've already made it this far and I can't very well walk back to my apartment in Manhattan from Brooklyn.

Wringing my fingers as I proceed, I feel the place oozing with sex and it makes me uncomfortable. I have no idea how I will make it through the entire night, but I find some small degree of comfort in the fact that no murderer would bring me into a club so filled with other people.

That's one good thing, right?

When the driver calls out to someone, I peer around him, gasping when my eyes spot the man in the picture. He's taller than I would have guessed, possibly six foot five inches , give or take an inch, and draped in an expensive dark grey suit, crisp white shirt, and a steel grey tie that matches the color of his piercing eyes. His physique is notable under his layers of clothing, solid, masculine and mouthwateringly sexy. His skin appears to be silky smooth, not a single blemish in sight.

His posture is straight—really straight, which shows his dominance and power and I can't help but swoon at the mere sight of him.

Fuck, he's even sexier in person.

"Jaxon, thank you. You may retire for the rest of the evening," Blake informs the driver, shaking his hand before turning to face me.

Dismissed, the driver walks away without so much as a second glance at me.

I am officially on my own.

"I hope the drive wasn't too long."

I stand in front of him speechless, a lump forming in my throat as he slowly allows his eyes to roam over me. Feeling foolish, I glance away from him. "Not long," I lie, and quickly scan the room. His gaze is both overwhelming, and possessive, and I can't help but look away from him.

His hand suddenly comes up to clasp me around my waist, the contact sending electricity through me. I take a chance, glance up at him and find that his eyes are still fixed on me, showing nothing but desire, which makes his eyes appear even darker than they were just a moment ago

"Would you like a drink first?" he asks, suddenly releasing me. I sigh softly at the loss of contact, but simply nod my head in response to him. *This man is intense.*

Turning away, he leaves me standing alone as he makes his way across the room to the bar. My eyes restlessly shift around the room. I've never been to a place like this and I feel completely out of my element.

Shit, you aren't in Kansas anymore, Lane.

Everyone here seems so free and confident, and I am anything but that. I know Blake will figure me out soon enough, but I hope it won't matter much to him. *How hard can being a sub really be? Yes Sir, no Sir, more please... I had seen it all in the videos I'd watched online. Easy peasy.*

Now that I know what to expect, for all my paranoia on my way here, I do want to enjoy this experience, enjoy him.

I smile at the thought of what tonight will bring. Having had only two pervious sexual partners previously, I am as inexperienced as they come. I focused so much on my studies in high school and college that I hardly ever dated or had any friends. Tonight is the first truly spontaneous thing I've ever done, and that excites me.

Slowly wandering through the club, I take in the scenes before me. I'm completely fascinated as I watch how much freedom the other couples have. They're not shy, and they seem utterly unaffected by the fact that people are watching them. No, they seem to actually enjoy it, even crave it I stop in front of a red-haired woman on display and stare at the lovers as they play out their scenes.

A naked, freckled-faced woman hangs suspended from the ceiling, her creamy, long legs pulled apart into a seemingly uncomfortable position by leather straps. Seated, with her legs bent, there is a thick strap of leather supporting her ass. Each of her legs is held in place by this contraption, exposing her completely shaven, glistening pussy for all to see.

My face reddens as I peer in on what seems like an intimate moment between the woman and the man standing before her. Her partner, a tall, dark, shirtless, well-built stallion of a man, trails a long white feather against her reddened opening, causing her to squirm in both delight and torment as she begs him to take her.

Instead of obliging, he moves the feather from her throbbing pussy to her inner thigh, which seems to send her further ablaze. Dripping with need, she calls out to him, still begging, needing, wanting him inside of her. Each desperate wail for more of him causes my breathing to become shallower, the woman's pleas fueling her own desire, her master's and mine. I stare at the woman's face, which appears anguished with need as he continues to tease her ever so slowly.

I don't understand why, but I am completely flushed with desire as I watch this couple. Wet, and dripping with excitement, I continue to watch, my body throbbing under the fabric of my dress. My lack of underwear only turns me on even more. I want to be that woman in that moment, I need to know what it feels like to surrender completely to such a strong, confident, sexy man.

"Like what you see?" I hear Blake murmur from over my shoulder. I don't turn to face him, choosing   instead to keep on watching the couple.

"Actually, yes, I do."

BLAKE

The look on Alyson's face as I return to her with our drinks in hand, is absolutely titillating to see. Her lips are parted, her eyes are hooded and a beautiful shade of pink flushes her cheeks.

Fucking gorgeous!

I half expected that she would have taken off when I went to the bar to order our drinks. It's apparent that she is in way over her head, and that she doesn't belong in a place like this.

Yet, as I look at her growing desire as she stares at the exhibit in front of her, I groan. My dick twitches inside my pants as I notice her face flush with desire. Downing both shots, one after the other, I place the glasses down on a passing waitress's tray, my eyes never leaving Alyson.

She bites down on her lip and gasps aloud when the man finally makes contact with the woman's gleaming pussy.

Closing the short distance between us, I stand behind her. "So this," I whisper softly into her ear, her sweet perfume teasing my nose, "this turns you on?"

Fuck, she smells so good.

She doesn't respond, instead, she closes her eyes and allows her head to fall back against my chest as I grip her small waist.

Taking her hand, I pull her away from the exhibit, wanting to get her into my private room as quickly as possible. I've had enough small talk. I need to have her underneath me and don't want to waste another moment.

The air in the elevator is charged with the thick scent of lust, as we ride to the uppermost floor. Her eyes never lift from the ground, but I watch the rise and fall of the deliciously exposed mounds of her breasts, which are nearly spilling from her skin-tight red dress.

My eyes continue to roam over her voluptuous curves, her hips are rounded, and her ass is high, and plump.

She looks fucking amazing.

The elevator dings and I restrain myself from leaping out and dragging her to my room. I know she isn't experienced, and I curse myself for putting myself in a situation where I have to consider every move I make. I am used to taking the lead. Hard, fast, deliberate and unrelenting is what I am accustomed to.

"After you," I murmur, stepping aside to allow her enough space to move past me.

I watch as she slowly brushes by me, her sweet, flowery perfume teasing my nose as she does.

Shit, I love her fragrance, but I quickly purge my mind of the thought. Just one night. One fucking amazing night, I remind myself.

The top floor only has a few rooms compared to the twenty rooms on the second floor. This floor is reserved for special members only, partners and high rollers who want both exclusivity and discretion when they frequent the club.

The second floor is open to whomever wants to use it, while the rooms on the third floor are assigned.

The red carpeted floor runs in three separate directions when you exit the elevator, the left and right corridors each lead to four rooms, but the one corridor straight head is my personal suite, one of the perks of being a partner.

As I walk up to the door and place my right hand in my pocket, I notice how apprehensive Alyson is at my side. Her eyes are wide, and she's biting down on her bottom lip revealing how nervous she is at the thought of what will happen once we cross the threshold and enter my suite. I can't help but smile inwardly as I swipe my access card and open the door wide for her to enter.

She steps inside tentatively, her eyes darting to cover every inch of the room, and I watch as an air of relief washes over her.

What exactly was she expecting? I wonder, as I close the door behind us.

Studying her as she moves around slowly, I watch as her fingers graze every surface as she passes. I know she's intrigued by what goes on here in the suite and I… I am intrigued by her.

She looks over to the open stainless steel and dark wood kitchen to her right, the all black living room before her, and she finally stops in front of the black stained wood mantel over the fireplace. Her hand lifts to the framed photo on the mantel, and she smiles at the familiar picture.

My eyes fall to her smile. Her full, desirable lips call out to me, luring me to slowly walk over to her. I want nothing more than to peel her out of the sinful dress she's wearing, take her hard, fast and wild, but I fight to remain in control of my urge.

There is a battle waging within me. The need to have her is stronger than I have ever experienced. Though I know she will eventually give herself to me, I can't help but yearn to speed up the process. Still, I take a calming breath.

Control. Stay in control, I command myself, hating the eagerness within me.

"Would you like a drink?" I ask, just as I step behind her. Her perfume still teases my nose, causing my groin to clench.

Fuck.

ALYSON

Do I want something to drink?

It's a simple question, one that I should be able to answer, but the teasing feel of his breath against my ear makes me suddenly incapable of voicing a response one way or the other.

I slowly turn to face him, hoping that not having his body pressed up against my ass will return my ability to speak. But, as I look up into his hooded, lustful, grey eyes, my breath hitches and all I can do is shake my head in response.

I don't want a drink, I just want him. I need him to show me what being with a real man is like. I want to finally understand what all the fuss is about sex.

I have denied myself the pleasures of being with other men for far too long, only focusing on my studies and keeping to myself. Were it not for two short-lived relationships back in high school, I would be a 22 year old woman who was still holding her v-card and who had never experienced an orgasm.

The latter of those possibilities is true. I have never experienced an earth-shattering orgasm, certainly not like those I've read about in romance novels. I've never known what it's like to forget my name in ecstasy underneath the solid, hard body of a sexy man.

No, I've been with boys; two boys who barely knew what they were doing in bed. Two boys who finished their business almost as soon as they started, leaving me unsatisfied and regretful that I had even bothered to be with them. They had been average, boring and totally uninspiring. But this man, now standing before me, is sinful, hot and mine for the night.

His eyes stare into mine with such intensity that my legs begin to tremble. That look alone has me panting with need.

Swallowing hard, I know that soon he will take me, and I hope like hell that afterwards I will be able to stomach the thought of leaving this place without him. The few short moments I have spent with him have already been the most thrilling moments of my life.

"So, how many Doms have you submitted to?" Blake asks, in a raspy voice, his eyes never leaving mine.

Shit, what should I say?

I wasn't prepared for him to ask me about my prior experience, although, thinking about it now, I realize how silly it was of me not to expect his curiosity.

Just confess, Lane, a voice screams from within me.

I know that I should just tell him the truth, lay it all for him I want to, I really do. I want to put all my cards on the table and not have it matter to him that I am as green as they come about sex, and even greener than that when it comes to his *lifestyle.*

"Four," I quickly blurt out, unable to stop myself from lying to him. My lie is already out there before I can even register it saying it.

"Four? Interesting," he says softly as he pulls away, a glint now in his eyes.

Shit, has he figured me out already? I wonder, as I intently return his stare.

"Um... yeah... four," I meekly continue to repeat my lie, now avoiding direct eye contact with him.

He moves to the black leather couch in the middle of the living room and sits down, a knowing smirk on his face as he looks back at me.

Shit! He knows.

BLAKE

Why she continues to lie to me, I haven't a clue, but I can't help but enjoy the look of panic on her face. *She is a defiant one*, I realize, loving the thought of teaching her a lesson about telling lies.

Deciding to have a little fun with her, I hiss. "You know, Alyson, lying to me when you have agreed to submit to me tonight isn't very wise," I inform her, keeping my voice deep and husky.

Alyson wrinkles her nose as her face reddens, and says, "And just what makes you think I'm lying?" she demands, her hands now balled into fists at her sides.

Shaking my head, I try hard to keep from laughing out loud, and comment, "All right then." With that, I stand up and walk away from her, leaving her standing alone in the living room. I will challenge her, make her confess her lie, and she will be underneath me when she does.

"Take off your clothes. Keep the heels on," I command her from over my shoulder as I stroll into the bedroom with determination. I hear her huff, but ignore her, chuckling to myself instead. She's cute.

We'll soon see just how long she'll stick to that story.

Freeing myself from my necktie, I go to the chest. Opening it, I look over all my tools, licking my lips as I imagine using each one of them on her. Reminding myself that I only have tonight with this defiant beauty, I want to choose wisely. My hands brush over my trusty flogger, tempting me to paint her fleshy ass red, but I decide against using it.

Releasing a groan, I close the chest sharply, the sound echoing in the spacious room. Damn! None of these instruments seem appropriate for Alyson. For the first time in my experience, I can't seem to find a fitting instrument, and I don't like the way that feels.

Fuck it. I know just what I have to do and I'm tired of wasting time.

Rolling up my sleeves, I stride back into the living room to the woman who has been throwing me off my game all night, stopping short as soon as I reach her.

I can't breathe. My lungs tighten and I feel as though I've been knocked off my feet, with the air sucked out of my chest, as my eyes fall to her round, perfect breasts, her peaked, stiffened nipples, and her soft milky skin.

Shit.

Her eyes are downcast. She is clearly embarrassed, but she has nothing to be ashamed of. She's perfect.

God, is she ever perfect.

"Look at me," I command with a strained voice, slowly making my way closer to her. She does as she is told, raising her head until her eyes meet mine—beautiful, crystal blue eyes that reveal her innocence and vulnerability.

Reaching out to her, I bring my hand up to cup her cheek. She stiffens beneath my touch, but slowly relaxes against my palm. I don't want to, but I know I should ask, given her inexperience, "Do you want to stop?"

She looks up at me, her eyes searching mine. I'm not sure what she's looking for, but she's searching for something... something that will help her decide.

Apparently finding the answer she needs, she nods her head just once, her eyes still fixed on mine, her chest rising and falling as soft, panting breaths are slowly released through her plump, slightly parted lips.

Her lips are perfect and I cannot help but picture them wrapped around my cock, milking me until I've emptied myself inside of her mouth. My cock twitches at the thought.

"I... I don't want to stop," she replies with a stutter, just before I take those gorgeous lips with mine.

"Good girl," I whisper, not breaking away from her.

Good fucking girl.

ALYSON

Holy shit, he tastes amazing!

Running his tongue across my bottom lip, he deepens the kiss, his hungry tongue tangling with mine. I don't deny him. Breathlessly, I open for him, allowing him to devour me.

His hands grip my hips possessively, and my body practically liquefies in his arms. Hot, wet and scorching, he continues to caress my tongue with his, setting my body ablaze. I have never before felt such heat, such intoxicating passion. He is suddenly everywhere, his hands gripping, pulling and tugging at every part of me.

"Too many clothes," I manage to gasp, when he finally pulls away, his own breathing labored. Not wanting to stop, I reach up to unbutton his shirt but he stills my hand.

"Not yet," he murmurs. "Go into the bedroom. Lie on your stomach and place your hands above your head," he orders, his eyes scorchingly hot with desire.

Gulping, I begin to move past him, knowing that the serious stuff is about to happen. I've completely forgotten about this part—the part where I pretend to like pain, and enjoy it when he orders me around.

"Yes, sir," I whisper, passing him as I walk down the hall to the only room with an open door.

Stepping inside, I am surprised to find that this room looks just like any other bedroom. From the images I have seen online, I half expected to walk into a torture chamber with hanging contraptions similar to the device from which the redhead downstairs had been suspended. Instead, I find a king sized four-poster bed covered with comfortable down bedding, a chest in the corner of the room and not much else.

Of course, he doesn't live here, it's a sex club.

Climbing onto the bed, I position myself as he ordered, lying on my stomach with my hands raised up above my head. I begin to place my head on the soft pillow but quickly decide to push it away, unable to block the mental image of how many other women Blake has brought here to this very bed and made to do this very thing. Gross!

Still, I lie there silently and wait, for what, I have no idea. I don't know what the heck he will have me do, but I know that I need it all. I want to experience this, although it also frightens me a bit.

Hearing him step into the room, he says nothing, but I feel his gaze upon me. There is something about the way he looks at me, as though I'm an unattainable treat he wants to both devour and protect at the same time. Never has a man looked at me this way before and it makes me feel special.

I hear him shift behind me and I stiffen up. I can't see him, but then I feel his hand softly caress my naked ass, as his other hand strongly grips my hip, and I can't help but moan aloud at his touch.

"I'm going to ask you again Alyson, just one more time. How many Doms have you served?" His voice is both husky and stern in tone.

I contemplate lying again, not wanting to give into him, but I know he will never believe me. Something has already set off his truth antenna and nothing I say will change that. It's time for me to confess.

He continues massaging my ass, making it hard for me to think clearly, but I release a sigh and finally admit the truth, "Just one. Only one... you," I murmur.

His hands still as I hear him release a ragged breath. *Is he going to ask me to leave now?*

He clears his throat after what feels like forever, his hands completely leaving me. "Lesson number one, Alyson, never lie to your Dom. Do you understand?"

I simply nod my head, in acknowledgement.

"Words Alyson. I need words," he says, his tone of voice holding a warning.

Gulping, I respond, "I... understand."

"You understand, Sir," he commands firmly.

"I understand, Sir," my voice is soft as I respond. I don't know where this will lead tonight, but I know that I need this desperately.

Seemingly satisfied, his hands return to masterfully caress my bottom, as I relax into the bed.

"Your safe word?" he asks, his voice still carrying a note sternness.

Safe word? Shit, I think I remember what that's for. Think, think, think…

"Um, stop?" I ask, unsure.

Blake chuckles sarcastically behind me, "Really clever."

I can't help the sting I feel in my heart. I don't want to feel hurt by his comment, but I just can't help it. Pushing myself up onto my knees, I climb out of bed, now wanting to get away from him. Obviously, this is all just a joke to him.

"I think I should go," I murmur, willing the tears welling up in my eyes to remain at bay. I won't allow myself to break down and cry in front of him. I know I'm a fool to have ever agreed to this date, but as least I will leave with my head held high and my dignity intact.

So man the hell up, I order myself, as I dart toward the living room for my clothes. *A fucking joke. I am just a fucking joke to him.*

"Alyson, where are you going? What's wrong?" Blake asks, as he follows me to the living room, his hands reaching out to grip mine.

I close my eyes, continuing to will away my tears. I should have known this would happen.

"Nothing's wrong. This was obviously my mistake. I'm sorry to have wasted your time," I whisper, my eyes still closed.

"Why are you leaving?" he persists, his voice softening, his concern evident.

Opening my eyes, I look at his face, noticing his tenacious and troubled gaze, and his raised brow. "Would you please just call for a cab?"

BLAKE

I'm in no hurry to call for a cab, or for this evening to end. I don't release her right away. Instead, I continue to stare at her, trying to understand what could possibly be going on in her head. This bullshit about her not belonging here isn't cutting it. She knew that before she even arrived.

So what changed?

"Shit," I groan when it finally hits me—it's my laughter. That's what has her running for the hills. I laughed at her.

"Alyson, look…" I trail off as I pull her closer to me, her hands still clutching her clothes to her chest.

God, she is beautiful.

"I didn't mean to upset you. I didn't think…"

"It doesn't matter, Blake. Really, it's fine. Just call for a cab," she cuts me off, the look on her face clearly indicating that she's obviously anything but fine.

Shit, this is exactly why I don't want to deal with a novice. It's why I have only placed ads seeking experienced subs, and why I have never slept with an only-vanilla partner.

Grasping her hand, I begin to pull her back toward the bedroom, no more questions or fucking feelings. She came here to get something from this experience, and I will gladly give it to her before I send her away.

I inwardly groan at the thought of sending her away, but I know it's the best choice, since she's too much trouble for me to deal with. Nothing about this night has gone as planned. Not even her punishment, which I am just about to skip entirely.

"What are you doing Blake? Call a cab for me now!" she yells in protest, as we reach the bedroom.

Ignoring her demand completely, I quickly spin her around and take her lips, successfully shutting her the fuck up.

Fucking aggravating as hell, this woman. But shit, she tastes amazing. Sweet as candy.

She doesn't protest my kiss much at all, leaning into me and dropping her clothes to the floor and placing her hands around my neck. The feel of her teasing fingers against the back of my neck sends me over the edge. I need to be inside of her.

Lifting her up and placing her legs around my waist, I push her back against the door, taking her pink, deliciously peaked nipple into my mouth. She moans at the sensation of my tongue lapping at her.

She pulls and tugs at my shoulders; panting heavily with each suckle. I watch her unravel in my arms, completely at my mercy. I love the look of pure ecstasy on her face. She's breathtakingly beautiful and her body hums under my ministrations.

Taking her other nipple in my mouth, I nip and lap at it, repeating the treatment I gave the other nipple, as she yelps and moans in response. Her legs tighten around my waist and I know she is on the edge.

Not wanting to waste another moment, I carry her to the bed and set her down. I take a moment to admire her hooded gaze and flushed skin, her desire for more evident on her face.

"On your back, now," I half pant, my own desire fully ignited. I can't recall any other time when I've felt so desperate to be inside of a woman... a time in which I've wanted nothing more than to give her what she needs. But this woman shows up and suddenly everything about my plan for tonight has gone to shit.

I won't like how I'm handling this tomorrow. I know that I will think myself weakened by it, but at the moment, I simply don't give a shit.

She does as she is told, lying down on her back, her breathing is still erratic and labored. I go my chest and pull out a red silk scarf. "I'm going to blindfold you now," I inform her, not wanting to alarm her any more than I already have.

ALYSON

"Okay?"

I don't mean for it to sound like a question. Blake is intimidating, powerful and panty-meltingly sexy. The way he just took control and kissed me despite my little meltdown was so incredibly hot that I couldn't resist him.

Even now, his ordering me to lie down on the bed turns me on. I am beginning to understand this whole taking orders thing. There is nothing sexier than a man who knows exactly what he's doing and looking fucking hot as he's doing it. Blake is all that and more.

He climbs onto the bed, straddling me. Leaning over me, he places the silky red blindfold over my eyes and ties it tightly behind my head, taking away my sense of sight. Plunged into darkness, all I can focus on now is my thundering heart beating wildly inside my chest.

"Just relax. Focus on what you feel," Blake's voice soothes, his hands trailing softly down my chest. His soft fingers leisurely trail across my aching breasts, causing me to shiver beneath his touch.

I feel him shift on the bed, his chest now presses against my aching core and I groan at the contact. My hands start to reach for him, but he pins them at my sides.

"Don't move," he orders, and I still almost immediately, not wanting him to stop. His lips descend to my breasts, his tongue masterfully working my stiff and aching nipples. I moan and arch my back, wanting more, as he suddenly nips hard at the tender peaks, causing me to yelp out loud.

He immediately soothes the sting, blowing softly over my nipples, and lapping at them again with his tongue, taking the pain away before he nips at them again. Over and over, sharp pain and then a soothing touch, each time causing my body to flood with unrelenting desire, ablaze in sensitivity. What he's doing to me is electrifying and I want more. "Please!" I cry out, my hands gripping fistfuls of the comforter beneath me.

He releases my tender nipples, slowly trailing soft kisses down my body, to the apex of my thighs, descending further until… Oh God," I cry, as he takes my clit into his hungry, eager mouth. I arch up into him, needing more.

"Please Blake," I beg, as he unrelentingly bites and suckles at my small bundle of nerves. The pressure between my legs steadily increasing with each passing moment.

"What do you want?" he rasps out against me, never breaking his masterful assault on my senses.

"Please… I… need," I stammer, as he works my body to the edge of something that feels completely foreign to me, my body beginning to tremble against his skillful tongue. "Oh God!"

"Say it! Tell me what you want," he growls, releasing me just before I explode, causing me to whimper in protest.

"Fuck me!"

BLAKE

That's all I need to hear. Those two words falling from her perfect pink lips set off something inside me, something primal, and all I can do is give in to her demand.

Lifting her trembling legs up around my arms, I take a moment to look at her shaven pussy, dripping with desire. *Perfect, just fucking perfect.*

I plunge deep inside of her with a single swift, brutal thrust, causing her to squeal in surprise, as a loud gasp bursts from her throat. Holding her hips, I can't help but groan at her body's tight hold around my cock.

Shit, she's going to fucking destroy me. She feels too good.

Giving her a moment to adjust to my invasion, I slowly pull out of her and then slam back into her to the hilt, filling her completely.

"Oh my God," she cries out, as she lifts herself up onto her elbows, her head thrown back, wild with the pleasure I'm giving her. Burying my head against the crook of her neck, I allow her sweet, delicious scent to fill my lungs and fuel my thrusts into her tight heat, each stroke more forceful than the last.

"Blake… oh God… I can't take it," she screams out, as I pound into her relentlessly, her long tanned legs wrapping even more tightly around my waist, begging for more.

Her hands come up to surround my neck, her fingers digging deliciously into my skin. Panting, yelling, and begging, she grinds herself up against my thrusts, meeting me each time and bringing us both closer to release. The sounds of our grinding hips, the slapping sounds of our bodies coming together and her breathless, pleasure-filled moans fill the room. The most beautiful sounds that have ever graced my suite all come from her.

Her sweet, wet pussy clamps tightly around my cock, signaling that she is close to her release, but I'm not yet ready for this to end. I swiftly pull out of her tight grip, ignoring her pleas of protest. Panting, I stare down at her, completely amazed.

She is nothing like I imagined and everything I wanted. She is fucking perfect. The perfect sub, despite her constant defiance. And she doesn't even fucking know it.

"Why did you come here tonight?" I ask, my voice strained and breathless as I pull off her blindfold.

She just looks up at me, her eyes are barely open, and confused. I don't know why it matters to me. I have never cared before, but I want to know, I really need to know.

She looks away from me, her eyes suddenly filled with sadness. "I needed to know what it was like," she whispers, her voice small.

"What did you need to know?" *Did she just want to use me as I'd initially planned to use her?* I wonder, suddenly not liking the thought of that at all. She doesn't answer my question. Instead, she scoots up into a sitting position on the bed, her eyes avoiding my tenacious stare.

"Rule number one," I remind her, firmly.

Nodding her head, she lowers it before answering, "I needed to know what an orgasm felt like—I've never experienced one before."

She's ashamed, as though something is wrong with her instead of the pussies she's been with before. They were obviously incapable of bringing a woman pleasure. Understanding her better now, I pull her body without warning until she's again lying flat on her back on my bed.

When she opens her mouth to speak, I cover her lips with mine, forcing my tongue into her mouth as I simultaneously reclaim her still drenched pussy with one forceful thrust.

She yelps her surprise into my mouth, sinking more deeply into the bed, and allowing her pleasure to take over.

I can't explain it, but I want to give her this. This entire night has been about nothing but her. I need to give her the experience she wants, show her just how much pleasure her body is capable of experiencing. Tomorrow we will part ways, but tonight, and just for tonight, I need to forget about what I want and be her Dom, the one to take care of her needs.

"Come for me, Alyson. Give in to the pleasure," I growl, my hands snaking between us, never breaking our kiss, as I begin to rub her slick and swollen clit.

She writhes underneath me, clawing at my back as she suddenly cries out, giving in to the power of her release, her body pulsating, and humming with fierce, intense pleasure.

ALYSON

"Oh my God. Blake!" I cry out, as he thrusts strongly inside me, rolling his hips against mine to prolong the scorching hot, fiery pleasure as it courses through me.

This is it… the moment I've read about in all those books that fill my bookshelf. This is what it feels like to lose yourself completely in heated passion with another person. I want to scream, yell, curse, pull, grip and tug away at him as I bask in the blazing glory of the ecstasy he's giving me.

I never want it to end, I never want him to stop. I want to bottle up this moment up so that I will never forget this night, the night I feel sexually awakened for the first time. It is as though I were dead before, living, but not alive—not truly. I existed, never fully experiencing the moments that might have shown me the joys that were possible in this world. Tonight I finally feel free, as Blake continues his assault on my throbbing, aching, and greedy pussy, and I never want to be caged again.

"You feel so fucking good," Blake growls, looking deeply into my eyes, as a fresh surge of excitement begins to build within me. Clamping down on his cock, I roll my hips to match his pace, desperate for the imminent release I am sure he'll soon give me.

Skillfully, he spears me deeper, harder, and faster until I'm sure that I am going to explode. A guttural growl rips from Blake's throat as his impending release nears mine, until finally we burst into the wet, white hot fire of orgasm together, his eyes never leaving mine.

Panting breathlessly, he collapses on top of me, sweaty, and musty, and delicious.

This man has just given me something I will never forget, and in this moment I want desperately for the night to never end, but as I slowly come down from my blazing release, I realize that it must.

"That was…" he stutters, his breath still heavily labored.

"Fucking amazing?" I finish, a wide smile planted on my lips.

It's the best experience of my life, but I am not going to tell him that. It's bad enough that I had to admit to the man that I'd never had an orgasm. How embarrassing.

He rolls over and stands up from the bed as a flood of curses escape his lips. Confused, I instinctively sit up on the bed, pulling the covers up around me.

"What's wrong?"

He doesn't answer me right away; instead he rakes his hands through his hair.

"Condom. The contract. Everything," he states matter-of-factly, as if I should somehow understand what the heck he is talking about.

When I don't respond, he turns to face me. "I'm sorry. It's just I've never..." he trails off.

Understanding, I offer, "Me either, but I'm on the pill, if it matters." He seems to relax at that admission, but still makes no move to get back into bed.

Suddenly it occurs to me that he is probably ready for me to leave. Climbing out of bed, I make a move to head toward the living room to fetch my clothes, yet not really wanting to think about leaving, fearing that I will feel... I'm not sure what I will feel, but I know I won't like it.

"What contract?" I ask, just as I reach the bedroom door.

"It doesn't matter now, I guess," he murmurs, shaking his head.

BLAKE

I don't want her to leave, but with this fuck up, I know that she should. How the fuck did I forget to wear a condom or have her sign a contract?

Tonight went completely out of control. Heck, I went out of control, and I can't even begin to wrap my head around it. Alyson has somehow managed to derail me, causing me to behave completely out of character and I can't have that. I can't allow another woman to destroy me. Not again.

Strolling to the living room, I find her already dressed and waiting. Her face and her body language have reverted back to the insecure woman she was when she first arrived at The Dungeon.

I try to ignore the pang of guilt I feel at causing her to feel that way, knowing that this part of the evening is difficult for her. The women that I've normally entertained here know what this arrangement entails, but Alyson is innocent, pure and adorable.

Sighing, and knowing that I will regret the next words to come out of my mouth, yet incapable of stopping myself from saying them, I tell her, "I'll take you home."

It isn't something I usually offer. Jaxon, my driver, normally drives the women home or they opt to take a cab. But, since I have foolishly given Jaxon the night off, and I sure as hell don't want to hand Alyson over to a strange cabby, I have no other choice.

She nods, picks up her purse and proceeds to the door. Just before she reaches it, she turns to face me. Her eyes have such a look of sadness, and a war wages within me.

Tell her to stay the night, at least.

God, I want to tell her to stay. Fuck that. I want her to never leave. I'd rather tie her to my bed and fuck her for the rest of my life, but she is a dangerous piece of business, although she doesn't even realize it.

No, I definitely need to take her home.

"Thank you for tonight," she whispers softly, before leaning into me, and planting a soft kiss at the corner of my mouth.

She's thanking me? I am fucking letting her walk out of here and she's thanking me. Way to fucking twist my gut into a knot.

"I'd better get you home," I respond, keeping my voice even and seemingly unaffected, although I am anything but.

ALYSON

The drive back to my home doesn't seem nearly as long as did the drive to the club. The roads are mostly empty, providing us with clear passage.

Blake hasn't said a single word to me during the entire drive, and even now, as he pulls up in front of my apartment building, he is deathly silent.

Should I say something? Should I just climb out of his car and walk away, never looking back?

When the car stops, I figure there is really nothing left for me to say. The night has been long, eventful, but long nonetheless, and we both knew that this part would eventually happen. I wish it didn't feel so damn awkward.

Opening the car door, I climb out, ready to walk away from him and take with me the precious gift he's given me. I will never forget it. I'm not sure why, but I know that he hadn't given me the same BDSM treatment he would have given any other woman who might have answered his ad. In fact, he behaved more like a boyfriend, catering to me, and making sure that I experienced what I'd come for. I know that I will never forget it or him, and I know with certainty that will never find it again.

But it is better to have it and lose it, than to never have had it at all, right?

"Wait," I hear him say, as I start making my way to my apartment door.

Turning, I see him climb out of his car, a BMW that still has that brand new car smell.

Reaching me, he pulls me into him without warning, sweeping me into a steamy, scorching kiss before releasing me. "You are welcome," he smiles, and I can't help but smile back at him.

"See you around, Blake."

Turning away from him, I walk into my building and release the breath I've been holding as I hear him peel off and drive away.

Damn he's hot.

I am going to miss him, I realize, as I walk inside my apartment, throwing my keys and purse down on the kitchen table before pulling off my ridiculously high heels.

Smiling, I peel off my dress, tossing it into the hamper and turning on the hot water in the shower.

Do I feel sad that the night has ended? Maybe. Will I ever regret it? Not for one second. Because Blake Hanson gave me something I will forever treasure. He freed something inside me that I hadn't even known was there in just one night.

AN EROTIC ROMANCE

JUST ONE
Night

VOL. 2

ALYSON

Holy crap, I just had my first real orgasm!

I'm grinning from ear to ear at the realization that I finally feel like a real woman. I happily step into the steaming hot bath, allowing the jasmine bath salts I added to work out the delicious aches left in Blake's wake. I never realized how exhausting and strenuous sex could be. Then again, I never had sex with anyone like Blake before. And boy, did it surpass any and all of my expectations!

You slut!

Yes, it was slutty of me to go out with this stranger for the sole purpose of having sex with him, but damn it, having now experienced everything I've been missing, I would do it again… and again... and, oh yeah, again!

With a shit-eating grin, I can't help but remember his sizzling touch, his smoldering steel gray eyes, and the way he took complete control over my body, setting it gloriously ablaze.

God, he was perfect. Just fucking perfect!

It had been an impeccable night, despite the minor hiccups, but I wasn't silly enough to believe that he had given me more than a fraction of the same treatment he'd have given a more experienced sub—the videos I watched online told me that much. Instead, he had been compassionate when needed, rough when necessary, and purely animalistic as he brought my body to heights it had never known.

Why did he take it so easy on me? I haven't the faintest idea, but I loved every second of it.

Leaning back in the bathtub, I close my eyes, only to imagine his darkened, feverish, eyes staring at me, drinking me in. I can't help but moan as I allow my hands to roam over my body, mimicking his touch as I experienced it, just an hour ago. It doesn't feel the same, lacking the equivalent excitement that his touch provided, but it's all I have now. I will never see him again; never experience his heart-stopping kisses, his alluring stare.

Will I miss him?

The question can't be answered, at least not while the memories of the night are still so freshly imprinted on my mind. But I push the thought away nonetheless, not wanting to worry about the potential damage I've opened myself up to by allowing this man, this sex-god, to have his way with me, only to have him walk away afterwards.

Bringing my right hand up to cover one of my still swollen breasts, I slowly caress it, imagining his skilled tongue lapping over it, elongating it, just as he had nipped at and suckled on my peaked nipples. I whimper at the thought, as my left hand descends down my body to the place that still yearns for his filling. Finding my clit, I rub it in slow, torturous circles, my breath quickening as the throbbing between my legs steadily increases. My thoughts are only of him and how he completely filled me, lusciously stretching me, and increasing the fire within me. Maintaining the same pace, I bite my lip as my mind drifts back to how forcefully he'd repeatedly thrust into me.

No one else is going to fuck you like that. That man is one of a kind, Lane.

Saddened by the thought, I pull my hand from between my legs, my desire suddenly gone. How can I miss a man I barely know?

Climbing out of the bath, I grab the plush, warm robe hanging behind the door and wrap it around myself, protectively. I know it's silly of me to feel saddened at the thought of never seeing Blake again, and I can't help but wonder what it would be like if I'd met him under different circumstances. Would he have been open for more? Am I open for more?

Get a grip! You fucked! It was amazing, but now it's over. Move on!

Deciding that my conscience is right, I shake my head in an attempt to free myself of all thoughts of Blake—at least for now. It was one night. One ab-so-fucking-lutely wonderful night, and I need to appreciate it for what it was and then move the hell on.

A soft knock at the door startles me out of my reverie.

Who the hell is that? I wonder, as I make my way to the door, grabbing the bat I keep near the entryway. I'm not normally a paranoid person…well, no more paranoid than I would consider normal, but, since I live all alone in New York City, without even a single friend to call on, I always keep a weapon of some kind near my door, just in case. This metal bat once belonged to my father, and having it there for protection always makes me feel as though he's there for me if ever I need protecting, such as right now when I'm about to open the door for God knows who at this very late hour. I am painfully aware of my vulnerability, but I continue on, although I fear it might be a rapist.

Yeah, because rapists are known to knock on your door before they steal your virtue! What the hell, Lane?

I push that ridiculous thought out of my mind. No rapist or murderer is going to knock on the door. I chastise myself, but I still I hold onto my sidekick metal bat. I have either been living in New York City for far too long, or my obsession with *Law & Order* has turned me into a paranoid mess. Twice tonight, I've turned a simple situation into a scenario in which I end up raped and murdered.

"May I help you?" I call out through the door as I look through the peephole, not wanting to open it, just in case my fear hasn't been ridiculous after all. I listen for a response, but I don't hear or see anyone out there.

Curious still, I slowly unlock the deadbolt, taking a deep breath before finally pulling the door open, my bat resting against my left shoulder, ready to take out any threat.

Holy fuck, I gasp, as my arm relaxes from its batting stance, the bat now loosely held by my right hand.

BLAKE

I made it all the way to the Brooklyn Bridge before turning the car around. Thoughts of Alyson fill my mind, drawing me back to her place.

The night isn't over, I think, as I make my way back to her apartment.

It has only been a half-hour since I left her. I'm not sure what I'll say to her once I arrive, but I cringe at the eagerness within me as I exit the car and rush to the front door of her building. I have never done anything like this before, and I know that come morning, I'll probably regret running back to her in the middle of the night like an adolescent schoolboy.

I haven't felt this kind of pull within me in years, and my mind drifts back to a time when I was so lovestruck that doing things like coming back to see a woman after a date was the norm.

But this wasn't a date, and I wasn't that adolescent boy anymore. I'm older and smarter now, and I won't allow myself to ever be so weak again, or let any woman hurt me the way...

Not again, I remind myself, trying my best to convince myself not to go there.

But damn it, I just have to have Alyson for a little longer. A round two, so to speak. That shouldn't hurt me any.

As long as I'm not with her when the sun comes up, I am still keeping to my "one night only" rule, I tell myself repeatedly, as I scan the intercom to find her name.

She has already managed to derail me from all my rules. This one rule must be kept, no matter what.

Should I buzz her?

No, I decide, not wanting to give her the chance to deny me the opportunity to see her. Instead, I buzz someone on the floor directly above hers and wait for the person to answer.

"Hello?" A man's woozy voice comes over the intercom.

"Excuse me, but would you please buzz me in? I seem to have forgotten my keys. I'm in 5C."

The man curses softly under his breath but buzzes me in.

That is easy.

Taking the steps two at a time, I make it to her floor in no time, and even before catching my breath, I slowly knock on the door, eager to see her.

Fuck, what if she thinks I'm desperate?

When she asks who's knocking, I can't breathe. I'm still doubled over from running up the stairs and am still trying to steady my breath. Soon, however, she opens the door, and she's standing in front of me, wearing nothing but an oversized robe, which is hanging off her shoulder, and she's holding a metal bat in her hand.

Fuck!

"Blake? What are you... is everything okay?" Alyson asks, her brows furrowed in confusion.

Taking a deep breath, I stare at her, taking in her perked, swollen breasts, visible through the slight opening in her robe, her hair cascades across the soft exposed skin of her shoulder.

I don't answer her question. Instead, I close the distance between us. Her breath suddenly hitches in her throat as I softly push her back inside the apartment, kick the door closed with my foot, and claim her mouth with me in a matter of mere seconds.

No time to waste.

She doesn't protest; instead, she falls into me, allowing me to deepen the kiss. Our tongues dance sweetly and passionately as I turn her around, lifting her into my arms and pressing her body back against the closed door. My hips hold her in place as she wraps her legs around my waist. Taking the bat away from her without breaking our embrace I allow it fall to the floor before bringing my hands back to her, tugging on her robe, pulling it slightly off her shoulders, and feeling her silky, soft skin against my fingers.

Ah, so soft!

Pulling away, she pants harshly. "But… I thought you said just one night?" she asks, between breaths.

"The night isn't over yet, Alyson."

ALYSON

Holy shit, holy shit! Blake is in my apartment and he smells so fucking good... so hot.

I groan as my steady breathing changes to short panting breaths, excitement coursing through my veins. Grabbing fistfuls of his silky hair in my hands, I lose myself in his hungry kiss, feeling the need he has for... what exactly?

The man came back. Shit, you must have done something right, I think, as I and smile against his lips.

"Something you care to share?" he asks me, as he breaks away from the kiss, one eyebrow raised, seemingly in amusement.

I blush slightly, not sure whether or not I should share my thoughts with him. Surely, the rough and tough Blake can see the humor in his actions. Mr. A-contract-is-a-must has been a flustered mess all evening. Forgetting the condom, the contract, and, although I can't prove it, I am fairly sure that he doesn't normally drive his dates home after their encounters. Yet, he has done all those things with me tonight, and he did indeed come back to me, perhaps the most inexperienced submissive on the planet.

Balls to the wall, you might as well just go with it. You aren't going to see him again after tonight.

Feeling brave, I look at him, a smile still playing on my lips. "Did you miss me already, Blake?" I ask, in a teasingly playful manner.

His smile falls away, and he stares at me for a few moments, his face impassive, not giving me a clue away what he's thinking. I begin to regret my words as I wait for him to show a reaction, any reaction. Have I ruined the moment? Have I crossed some sub-line that I shouldn't have?

Unexpectedly, he sets me down upon my feet, his eyes never leaving mine as he does so. The thumping of my heart is all I can hear as we maintain eye contact until suddenly I remember reading an article online which states that a sub should never look her Dom directly in the eyes.

Who the fuck came up with such an archaic rule?

Ancient though as it might be, I don't want to disappoint him. I pull my eyes away from his, staring down at my hands closed and resting in front of me instead.

"No. Look at me," he finally commands, his voice harsh yet strained with some emotion that I can't quite place. I do as I am told, raising my eyes up to meet his, and feeling the sudden charge of electricity in the air between us, as his eyes darken, and his lips part, softly panting.

"The night isn't over yet," he groans softly, repeating his earlier words, although it seems he might have said it more for himself than for me. He swiftly takes my hand into his, turns quickly on his heels, and leads me back into my apartment.

His eyes wander to and fro, searching, until he spots my bedroom door, which was left ajar, and with my bed directly in his line of sight. Striding to the room with strong, purposeful steps, he enters, pulling me along behind him.

First man to ever step foot into your bedroom and you have your stuffed animals stretched out over your bed. Nice... just fucking nice. So damn sexy, Lane!

I cringe as I watch him intently, trying to gauge his reaction to my minimal space. The room isn't much; it contains a simple white iron twin bed, set in the very center of the room, with a baby pink comforter over it and matching curtains. My stuffed animals, which vary in size, lay against my pillows, roughly ten of them. The room appears to have been decorated for a toddler. Given the fact that I was only seven when I lost my parents, I did not want to part with many of the things from my adolescent years. I never dreamed that I would ever have such a fine, sexy specimen walk into this bedroom anytime soon.

Turning to face me, he drinks me in as I stare up at him expectantly, waiting for him to say or do something, anything. Blake peers down at me, his piercing gaze precipitously revealing the desire brewing within him, yet he seems hesitant to make a move. He's waiting, perhaps pleading?

Haltingly, I step close to him, laying my hands on his sculpted chest. His breath hitches at my touch, but it only encourages me to further my advances.

Shit. I am really doing this. I am going to seduce Blake in my damn bedroom—in front of Mr. Bear-Bear. God, I really need to redecorate this fucking room.

Slowly, I unbutton his shirt, my eyes still fixated on him. He doesn't stop me, and, when I have his shirt completely unbuttoned, he allows me to tug it off of him, letting it fall to the floor. Returning my hands to his chest, I place a line of soft kisses on his hard, chiseled chest, drawing a gasp from him, as I flick my tongue against his nipple.

Of course, I don't know what the hell I'm doing, but I suddenly feel drunk... drunk on the fact that he returned... just for me, even if it is only for tonight, something inside him was apparently unable to forget me.

BLAKE

Alyson is completely oblivious to the effect she has on me. It's evident in the way she looks up at me each time she plants a kiss on my chest, almost as if she's asking my permission for her to continue. The feeling of Alyson's tongue flickering against me is almost enough to make me push her onto the bed and fuck her until morning, but I still haven't yet decided on what I want to do with her.

Everything within me wants to dominate this woman, to spank her beautifully rounded ass until it's a deep, beautiful crimson as punishment for luring me back to her place, yet another part of me, the part that tended to her needs earlier, fears that I might scare her away. How have I reached such an impasse?

Stop fucking overthinking this, I chastise myself.

Taking a deep breath, I reach my decision.

"Too many clothes," I murmur to her, and she immediately stops dead in her tracks at the sound of my voice, a smile playing at her lips. I now know that she's recalling her own words to me earlier this evening.

"Take off your robe."

Slowly, I pace around her, drinking in her plump, full figure as she makes quick work of ridding herself of the oversized garment. She now stands before me, shyly, with her hands cupped in front of her.

"On your knees, Alyson," I hiss softly into to her ear, while standing behind her.

Alyson eagerly falls to her knees, and my groin goes taut at her immediate compliance. "Good girl," I purr, as I stop directly in front of her. She is so eager, so willing.

Her eyes remain downcast, but the steady rise and fall of her chest indicates just how much I affect her. She's excited, and I can already tell that she is wet for me.

"You have been quite a handful, Ms. Lane. Very naughty in the way you've distracted me tonight. What shall I do with you?"

She whimpers, and I have to fight my need to fling her onto the bed and bury myself inside her tight pussy again in response to that beautiful sound, submissive sound.

"Look at me."

She obeys my command without hesitation, her head coming up, her eyes meeting mine from behind her long lashes, to meet my intense stare, letting me see the desire stirring deep inside her hooded and beautiful, crystal blue eyes.

She licks her lips, causing my own eyes to fall to her perfect, now-parted lips. Bringing my hand up, I tug her hair back, and she gasps in surprise. I can't help but notice the intense longing in her gaze, her bottom lip now held between her teeth. She wants me... wants this.

"Don't bite your lips, unless you want me to take that sweet mouth of yours with my dick," I half-whisper.

She releases the moist pink flesh, never taking her eyes off of me.

God, she looks gorgeous, perfect in every way.

"So beautiful," I murmur, as I tug her up by tightening my grasp on her hair. "So damn beautiful."

She groans softly. "Do you know what I want to do to you?" I ask, as I move her closer to the bed. I watch as her breathing increases, her eyes are barely open, but her gaze is still intent on me and filled with her greedy, lusty desire.

She regards me silently before answering, "Spank me, Sir?"

Oh Alyson, Alyson.... So innocent, so right...

Pushing her softly onto the bed, I swiftly flip her over so that she is now lying on her stomach, my hands still tightly gripping her hair.

"I've been wanting to paint that creamy ass of yours red from the second you first walked into my club," I growl, as I slowly massage her tender flesh with my free hand.

"Ah, so smooth and soft. Do you want me to spank you, Alyson? To paint your fucking ass red before I fuck you again? Is that what you want?"

She moans, breathlessly, now panting, as I continued my ministrations on her plump, soft flesh.

"Words, Alyson. Let me hear you, darling," I tell her, stilling my hand on her behind.

Fuck! Say yes!

"Oh, God, yes," she moans, just before I bring my hand down, striking her fleshy round ass. She gasps in surprise as she inhales sharply.

She stills, but for only a moment, allowing the initial shock to ebb before she pushes her ass up against my hand.

"You like it, don't you?" I whisper into her ear, allowing my hot breath to tease her lobe until she whimpers softly.

I massage her now pink-tinted skin tenderly before lifting my hand to once again to strike against her flesh at a different spot.

This time she doesn't gasp; instead, she moans and tightly grips the comforter as she allows the sting to turn into pleasure, my hands helping, as I again knead her flesh.

Running my hands over her, I slide them down along her voluptuous ass and reach between her cheeks, through to her silky folds, plunging one finger into her warm, dripping pussy, only to be rewarded by her luscious wetness.

"You're so fucking wet," I whisper, as she releases a deep groan.

She whimpers again when I pull my finger out of her wet channel, causing me to smile down at her wanton state.

Perfect. She is perfect.

Without warning, I spank her again, harder this time, wondering just how much this woman can possibly withstand before she starts shrieking. To my surprise and amazement, she continues moaning in torturous pleasure before I can even begin to caress her now crimson flesh.

"Ah... harder," she cries out, as I repeatedly slap at her tender ass before kneading her stings away. Each time, she reciprocates by grinding against my hands, urging me on. Before long, she is shuddering beneath me, heaving and shaking as her arousal deepens.

"Blake... Sir, please," are her only words, and I can no longer hold back the need burning within me.

Take her, now! It's my only thought as I release her hair and back away from the beautiful sight before me.

She hadn't screamed bloody murder, hadn't cried endless tears, as I rained down blows on her soft, delicious ass. She enjoyed every moment of it, wanting to feel the delicious sting of my hand on her ass.

Slowly, I undress, leisurely unbuttoning my pants and slipping them off, as I peer down on this lovely woman, her reddened, sumptuous ass still displayed before me. She takes a sharply drawn breath at the sound of my clothing falling to the floor in anticipation, and I cannot deny that my anticipation of sinking deeply into her delectable folds also makes my heart race, eager to fill her again.

Placing my right arm around her torso, I hoist her body to the center of the bed, flipping her over, so that she now is lying on her back, giving me a view of her feverish eyes, which are fully dilated with passion.

It's a glorious sight to behold. Her smooth, silky soft skin is coated in a light sheen of sweat, and her breathing is rapid and uneven as she waits for me to take her.

And take her, I will.

ALYSON

Oh. My. God. That was… fuck… that was erotic as hell!

Those BDSM videos I watched didn't do justice to what just happened between Blake and me. I was certain that I wouldn't enjoy such a treatment, but damn, it was the hottest thing I've ever experienced—the sting of his hand coming down on my exposed ass, followed by the warm, soft caress of his hand, nearly had me coming apart at the seams, and that was even before the intrusion of his skillful fingers.

How can something that seems so demeaning actually feel so damned good? Maybe these submissive people really are onto something.

Blake knelt before me, peering down at me with a dark, unexplainable expression on his face. I'd have normally felt highly uncomfortable under such intense scrutiny, but the rise and fall of his heaving chest eased me.

He is trying to maintain his control, I realized, and I instantly felt empowered at the realization. *It seems I am not the only one to be completely awestruck at our sexual chemistry.*

Feeling thrilled at the thought that he could actually be this affected by me, I teased him, dragging my lip through my teeth, ever so slowly, as I gazed up at him through my lowered eyelashes.

Don't punk out on me now Mr. Hanson.

I'm not a confident woman. I'm not one to openly flirt with the opposite sex at all, but seeing him so... what is the word I am looking for?

Primal. No. Hungry... Yes! He is fervently hungry, with his desire so clearly expressed by the depth of his gaze, almost painfully so, as he fights to control himself.

A guttural groan suddenly erupts from deep within his throat as his eyes focus on my lower lip. Before I can even register what he's going to do, he's on top of me, capturing my mouth in a smoldering kiss, stealing my breath, and I am lost in his heat.

We are all hands, lips, and teeth, panting, moaning and groaning as we press our bodies deeper into each other. Feverishly, he explores my mouth, our tongues deliciously intermingling and setting my body ablaze.

Clawing at his arms, back and shoulders, I writhe beneath him, desperate for him to quench the burning ache between my legs. The throbbing pulse between my thighs increases with each twirl of his tongue, and I can't help but arch my hips up into his, silently pleading for him to end this torturous teasing. I keep my eyes closed when he releases my lips and nips at my jaw, his hands alternately tugging and gripping firmly at my breasts.

"Please, Blake…" I cry out, when he suddenly twists my nipple, sending a sharp sensation throughout my buzzing body.

Blake groans into the curve of my neck and suddenly plunges his cock inside me with such brutal force that I jerk up, my body arching. I cannot contain the sounds that are ripped from my throat. Mindlessly, I open my legs wider, trying to convey my need for more of him.

"Yes," I cry out, finally feeling complete as our two separate bodies become one.

"So wet… you're so fucking wet," Blake utters through his clenched teeth as he slams into me strongly, our bodies jerking with each thrust, as he fills me to the hilt.

Withdrawing almost completely, he then plunges his cock back inside me, and I scream out unintelligible sounds, lost in the feel of him. So thick and so hard, his girth is almost greater than I recall. He continues his assault, pounding into me with such controlled force.

Burying his face in the crook of my neck once again, he gently bites into my shoulder; the sting of pain coupled with the sweet, agonizing pleasure he is bestowing drives me right over the edge. I feel myself suddenly falling as my body ferociously contracts around him. He brings his hand down to my cluster of sweet nerves and expertly rubs his fingers against my nub. I fall apart in his hands, my voice hoarse from screaming his name over and over. Blake groans loudly, throwing his head back as he finds his own release.

"Fuck, Alyson."

He collapses breathlessly at my side, our gasps echoing throughout the quiet room. We lay there, each of us lost in our own thoughts while we come down from our orgasms as exhaustion settles in.

My last memory before sleep overtakes me is of Blake's strong arms pulling me closer.

BLAKE

It's been a week. One whole fucking week since my night with Alyson, and I still can't get that woman out of my head. She is like a contagion that's coursing through my mind and my body, overtaking every part of my days, my nights… hell, my entire fucking life. Except, she isn't the kind of contagion you run from, she's the kind you run to, just as I did on the night we first met.

Since then, I've cancelled two meetings with women who responded to my ad. I keep finding reasons to justify it, but deep down, I know what the cause is. Her!

Fucking Alyson. She is everywhere, suffocating me, haunting me.

Every time I close my eyes, it's her face I see, her cries I hear. Even the mirror betrays me, as it reveals to me every place where she clawed at my skin, marking me as hers.

Even now, she haunts my club, showing up in a skin-tight dress, her ample breasts nearly spilling out over the top. I know that it's all in my head, that she's somehow cast a wicked spell on me, and it's making me lose my fucking mind.

Crazy. I'm going fucking crazy, I just know it.

Staring across the first floor of 'The Dungeon', I imagine her casually strolling through the club, her ass swaying beneath her dress as she moves from one exhibit to the next, never lingering, just taunting me.

She'll stop for a few seconds in front of one exhibit, decide that she's not impressed, and then sway her way to the next. Each time I think it's her, she'll disappear, clearly never having been here to begin with. I know I'm losing it.

Fuck, I need a drink, I think, as I swivel around in my seat at the bar and order a bourbon. "Make it a double," I bark at the bartender, irritated.

"You look like shit!" I hear Derrick say behind me. Not bothering to turn to face him, I nurse my fresh drink and stare straight ahead. There isn't much I can say to him anyway.

He's right, I do look like shit.

I've looked like shit from the morning after my one night with Alyson. It was a bad idea for me to return to her place instead of going home. She has somehow managed to ingrain herself within my mind. I just can't seem to shake her loose, and it's starting to piss me the fuck off.

In my suite, the sheets and comforter still retain her intoxicating scent. The blindfold I used on her seems too much of a prize to be thrown carelessly back into the chest, so instead, I find myself folding it neatly and placing it in the pocket of my suit jacket.

Why? Who the fuck knows? Just as I also can't explain why I continue to transfer it into the pocket of each damn suit jacket I've worn this week.

"Look man, you're really acting strange, you're normally a strange dude to begin with, so you're now acting even stranger than usual. What's up, little bro'?" Derrick asks, as he takes the stool next to mine.

"Two minutes. You're only two minutes older, Derrick, and I am just fine," I grunt, before I down the rest of my drink and lift myself off the barstool.

Coming to 'The Dungeon' was a mistake. I realized it the second I walked in, but I wanted to prove myself wrong. As thoughts of Alyson continue to dance around in my mind, it's obvious that the club is the last place I need to be.

"Bullshit!" Derrick calls out behind me, as he follows me to the door. "This wouldn't have anything to do with a certain newbie sub, would it?" he asks, his teasing voice grating on my nerves.

"Leave it alone, Derrick. I should never have told you about her," I bark, not breaking my stride. My brother and I have always had a close relationship which was why I thought nothing of telling him about my situation with Alyson, but I am just now realizing that telling him was a mistake. He doesn't understand. He has never experienced the kind of hell I'm going though and he will never understand the seriousness of this situation.

Yes, I said it. Alyson is a situation. One I need to fix immediately.

Derrick isn't like me. Sure, he enjoys the entertainment at the club from time to time, but only when he's in between relationships. Deep down, Derrick is a true-blue monogamous—a "serial exclusive relationship" sort of man. From the time he was in high school, he's always going from one serious relationship to another, never taking more than two months off before again finding himself in yet another serious relationship.

I, on the other hand, can only account for one, and it was that relationship that shaped me into the man I am today. I have seen no point whatsoever in monogamy since then. I see no sense in putting oneself in line for the pain and agony that those kinds of relationships eventually lead to.

Never again.

"I'll see you tomorrow, Derrick, don't be late. Just because you're my brother doesn't mean you can show up whenever you want."

Sidling up next to me, Derrick places his hand on my shoulder. "You know, she's not her. What you went through," he stumbles on his words, casting his head down thoughtfully before continuing, "She's gone but you aren't."

I don't respond to him, although his words drive a hard, penetrating spear into my chest. He is right. She's gone, and she left me a shattered, jaded man—a man who cannot afford to allow another woman to cause me the same grief and pain again. In my brother's reminder, he verified what I already know. I need to find a way to rid myself of Alyson. Permanently!

ALYSON

"Damn it."

Pushing myself away from my desk, I rise to my feet and begin pacing back and forth in utter frustration.

I've been searching the Internet for the past week looking for work, but it seems as though every position listed requires more experience than I possess. How the heck can this be? I have no idea. I've taken several internships assisting elementary school teachers since I was still in high school, preparing myself for this very moment—the part of my life when I could step out into the real world and begin my career.

But these fuckers... these invisible butt-wipes, hiding behind their computer screens, laughing at all the newly-graduated education majors, wanting more. It boggles my mind when I see that employers now insist that you have experience outside of internships, but they won't hire you so that you might actually gain that experience.

Fucking bullshit!

Taking a calming breath, I check my account balance, knowing that it's been months since I last looked at the statements. The trust fund I received from my parents fifteen years ago has been my only source of income since I turned eighteen and was given access to it. I just know that if I don't find employment soon, I'll be screwed.

Sitting back down at the computer, I log into my account and groan when the screen loads; the reality of how dire my situation truly is glares back at me in black in white. I'm financially fucked!

Well, what the hell did you expect? College, meals, clothes, rent... that fifty thousand dollars couldn't keep you going forever!

I have less than four thousand dollars left of the trust fund money and my rent alone is fifteen hundred.

What the hell am I going to do?

Needing a break, I again push myself away from the desk and make my way over to the couch. I need to think of something fast, but, short of discovering a stash of mob money at my front door, I'm not sure what else I can possibly do but continue my job search. But the endless searching, day in and day out, leave me frustrated, depressed, and tense. Really tense.

I bet Blake could work these frustrations out of my system, really well. I shiver with need at the thought.

Blake.

It's been a week since our one night together, and I still remember the way he made my body sing. I can't help but smile as I recall what was the most amazing night of my life. I had never before experienced such pleasures... such glorious heights of passion, and it had all been because of him. But, true to his advertisement, it had been just for the one night. He made damn sure that he slipped away before the sun could rise on a fresh new day.

He hasn't sent me so much as a single text or email since then, and I can't deny feeling a slight pang of disappointment, although I don't regret a single moment of our night together. *I don't think that any woman could ever regret Blake. He is one fine, sexy man.*

The night following our... encounter—yeah, let's call it that—I sat in my apartment, completely bored out of my mind. I was thrust back into my plain and ordinary life, a life with no excitement, no friends, no relationship, and no Blake. Sadness has been tugging at my heart and no matter how hard I tried to keep busy and push the loneliness away, I just couldn't do it.

I cannot deny that I was enthralled by Blake's world. I was beyond fascinated by his taboo lifestyle, although our encounter was relatively mild compared to what I'm sure he's was used to. Still, I want to know more, experience more. For too long I've closed myself off to everyone and everything exciting, not wanting to open myself up to the adventures this world holds for those willing to grab those adventures by the horns. For too long, I've sought safety in my relationships—if you can even call my association with the two adolescent boys to whom given myself, *relationships*.

Since the death of my parents, I've been living in a cocoon, shielding myself from the pleasures this world can provide, depriving myself of the sensual touches and the deep, long strokes from a man like Blake, and I am so tired of it… tired of the fortress I'd unwittingly built around myself. And Blake, Blake awakened me to a whole new world of sexual pleasure.

Before I could stop myself from over-analyzing my actions, the night following my night with Blake, I found myself in a cab bound for Brooklyn.

It was insane, bold and completely out of character for me, but even though I knew this, being with Blake had shed a bright light on the dark, lonely life I had been living, and I just couldn't, nor did I want, to imagine returning to that life again.

"Where to, ma'am?" the driver asks in an African accent as I climb into the cab, dressed in a skintight dress and heels that make my legs seem a mile long.

Fuck, I don't have the address. Shit, shit, shit.

"Um… err… Brooklyn. I'll search for the address on my phone as you head toward the bridge." I then pull out my cellphone in search of any known sex clubs in Brooklyn.

Oh Google, please don't fail me now!

After ten minutes of searching, and a plethora of failed search attempts, I finally find the address and almost start cheering aloud in the back seat of the yellow cab in my excitement.

Refraining, of course, but still smiling like a schoolgirl, I give the driver the address before leaning back into the comfortable leather seat. I'm on my way to see Blake.

I had previously returned to the club a few times since our encounter, after paying the very hefty monthly membership fee—a fee I surely would not be renewing at the end of the month.

A monthly fee of three thousand dollars on the off chance that Blake will fuck you again... no, you're not a slut—much!

Even though it was expensive, given my current financial circumstances, I didn't care, I was only focused on seeing him again. Each time I entered the club, I hoped and prayed that Blake wouldn't be there with another woman, and thankfully, he wasn't. It both thrilled and surprised the hell out me, but I wasn't about to complain.

I never approached him though, instead, I wanted to test the patience of the sex god himself—something I thought of on the fly when I first arrived at the 'The Dungeon'. I never long lingered there very often either. Each time I felt his gaze on me, I disappeared behind whatever obstacle would shield me from his view, and I loved the excitement of the game I was playing.

Beaming, I devised the plan for tonight's adventure. I wouldn't stalk him as I had done on the previous nights, and I wouldn't disappear as soon as his heated, lustful gaze upon me proved to be more than I could withstand.

No. The games I'd been playing with Blake Hanson were brutal on my body. The ache he created that first evening was steadily growing stronger within me each passing night, and he had me dripping with desire each time I was in his presence.

I'm not sure what the fuck I thought I was doing. How did I turn into someone so bold in just one short week, I haven't got the faintest idea, but I do know it has everything to do with Blake, and tonight I will finally step out of the shadows. I just hope he doesn't turn down my offer.

Yeah, good luck with that.

BLAKE

"What's the status of the Denali amalgamation merger? Have we ironed out the final details?" I asked Derrick, who was seated casually on one of the two chairs in front of my mahogany desk.

"Actually, I have an appointment with them this afternoon; we should have everything squared away," he mumbles, as he stares down at his cellphone, not bothering to look up from the device.

Glaring at him, I roll my eyes and proceed to review the documents from my most recent client, Joseph Adinolfe, the successful C.E.O. of a technology firm, who is interested in buying out a struggling competitor's firm. The acquisition would be extremely beneficial to him, and, in turn, beneficial to our firm as well.

My brother and I started Hanson & Hanson Inc. just under five years ago, and we've acquired a powerful and impressive roster of clients in that time. Initially, it was just the two of us, but, after getting through our first year in business together, we've turned our little two-man operation into a huge, successful firm, now employing nearly two hundred attorneys, and opening five branch locations throughout New York State.

It's been our dream coming true, despite the obstacles we've tackled over the years, one of which occurred three years ago, when my life fell apart… all because of her.

Groaning inwardly, I force all thought of her out of my mind, focusing instead on the mountain of paperwork I still must get through before the end of business today. There is nothing to be gained by allowing my mind to drift into the past, nothing good will ever come of that, and it will most certainly not change the outcome of what had happened back then.

"And, we're back," Derrick blurts out, suddenly, bolting out of his leather chair, his expression happy and cheerful.

"What the hell are you blabbering about? Don't you have work to do? A meeting to prep for?"

He flashes me a megawatt smile before leaning over my desk with both of his hands firmly gripping the outer edges. "Samantha and I, we're getting back together."

"Oh…," I say simply, before returning my attention to my paperwork. I'm not about to congratulate the man on his fucking relationship, not when I know that soon enough, they'll be breaking up again only to repeat the process.

Those two are fucking hopeless.

"Oh? Is that all you're going to say?" Derrick smirks, folding his arms over his chest.

Here comes Mr. Sensitive.

"That's nice." I add, although I am unable to understand what the hell he wants from me. Samantha is nice, I guess, but I care very little about his relationships and I care even less about the girl he's involved with. She's his problem, not mine.

"Ever the romantic," Derrick murmurs, before turning around and strutting to the door. "Anyway, I have meetings to prep for."

"Yeah, yeah…"

My brother and I are polar opposites. While he believes in trusting that his heart is safe in the hands of Samantha, I know better. I've learned about trust the hard way. I was once the romantic sort, eager to woo the only woman I ever loved, but in the end she only caused me heartache and pain. She ripped away all the promises of a happy future in just one night, causing me double the misery.

My mind drifts back in time to Elizabeth, and to the night she changed my life—the night she tore away my heart and soul.

I shudder, not wanting to think about what might have been if only we had discovered the problems sooner. Dwelling on the past will do me no good, and thinking about my pain, is what turned me into the man I am today.

I am structured, ordered, and in control of everything and everyone I have allowed to take up residence in my life.

Except for Alyson.

She's the first woman to push me beyond my self-made boundaries, and it still grates my nerves that she has been able to encroach on my thoughts each and every night like a swift and unwanted intruder.

Glancing at the computer on the far right side of my desk, I contemplate replying to one of the many still unanswered responses to my ad. Surely, a night with another woman will free me from the tight grip of Alyson's allure.

Determined, I promptly swivel my chair around toward the computer, click the email icon on my desktop, and proceed to scroll through my messages.

No... no... Hell no... Ah... Chantal... Perfect.

ALYSON

Dressed in a very flattering pale pink dress and ultra-high, fuck-me beige stiletto, I gingerly walk into 'The Dungeon,' trying my best not to fall flat on my face in this impossibly tight dress and these sexy but incredibly uncomfortable heels.

The shit we women go through.

Shaking my head at the thought, I stroll to the elevator, my heart thumping just as fast and hard as it does every time I return to the sex god's playground. The anticipation of seeing him again thrills me and causes my pussy to contract, just from the mere memory of feeling him inside me.

The elevator pings, indicating that I have arrived, and I step out and begin the long walk to the lone door at the end of the hallway.

This is it, I think, as I reach the door, and, with a shaky hand, open it. He's either going to tell me to kick rocks and send me home or he'll accept the proposal I plan to offer him. I haven't given much thought to how I'll make my offer exactly, but, in keeping with how I first ended up here at the club, I'm going to wing it.

How hard can it be to seduce him?

Before I can ponder it further, I find myself standing in front of the same woman, the hostess, manning the reception desk.

"Ah, Ms. Lane. I trust that you have been enjoying your time here thus far," she acknowledges, as I hand her my useless driver's license—New Yorkers really have no need of them given the bountiful number of subway stations and the many taxi cabs roaming the streets in search of their next fares.

"I have, thank you," I acknowledge simply, not wanting to prolong our conversation.

Scanning the room briefly, I frown when I notice that Blake is nowhere in sight.

Has he decided not to come here tonight? Tonight of all nights?

"Here you are, Ms. Lane," the hostess says, as she hands back my license, after she's done swiping it into her computer system.

I place my license back into my clutch before beginning to roam through the room, just as I've done each and every night I've been here. But this time, I don't feel the heated and alluring stare of Mr. Blake Hanson upon me, as I make my way through the crowded room, attempting to appear as aloof as possible.

Stopping in front of one of the exhibits, I gape, wide-eyed, as a sweaty, potbellied man laps away at a tightly restrained brunette. She seems to be enjoying his... what the hell can I call it... *oral skills?*

Bile rises in my throat, and I know that I should probably look away, but it's just one of those things that make you want to poke out your eyes with the first available sharp object, but for some incomprehensible reason, you just can't seem to tear your eyes away. Gross!

Shuddering, I move on to the next exhibit, and this one is more pleasant... more erotic, and appropriate, well sort of.

A tall, slender, blonde woman, dressed completely in shiny leather stands before another woman, who is stretched out over a table on her stomach. Her legs are widespread and the woman standing over her holds a long paddle in her hand. It appears to be made of leather, but I can't really tell.

I smile shyly, as I peer at their intimate exchange, knowing precisely what the tall woman will do next. I've seen this done in the videos I watched, prior to my date with Blake.

I wonder if Blake has one of those paddles. Oh, maybe we can role play. I'll be the high school girl trying to get into a frat party and he can punish me for crashing it. I groan at the thought, remembering how it felt when he spanked me.

Who am I turning into? I wonder, flushing, as I watch the tall blonde stroke the back of her submissive.

"Hello. Lane, isn't it?" I hear, over my shoulder, the voice pulling me out of my thoughts and away from watching the display before me.

Abruptly, I turn, finding myself flush up against a wall of hard, solid muscle.

Graceful as ever... I scold myself for my clumsiness.

"Oh… Shit… Sorry," I stutter, embarrassed, my hands still spread up against his hard chest.

God, he's so firm.

"No apologies needed," he replies, in an amused tone. It's only then that I look up at him, my brows furrowed when I suddenly find myself face-to-face with Blake's chiseled jaw, his smooth, sexy face, and his intense gray eyes, which are fixated on me.

You've got to be fucking kidding.

Startled, I crane my neck up, examining his eyes and the blank look on his face. He clearly wasn't looking at me with his familiar, yearning gaze, the one I've come to enjoy each time he sought me out at the club. I was sure he had come to believe that he had been imagining my presence, since I'd disappear from view just as quickly as I appeared.

Has the game turned him off? I wonder, as I quickly push the thought away.

It doesn't matter. I'm not someone he can pretend he doesn't know, especially after the fact that he had returned to my apartment. We were strangers still, but he had seen me at my most intimate and vulnerable, and he managed to bring out something in me that I hadn't even know was there.

Anger instantly flares up within me and before I can stop myself, I find my hands pushing me off his chest and sending him tilting backwards unexpectedly.

"Something wrong?" he asks, once he regains his balance, and it takes everything within me not to push him back even harder.

How fucking dare he?

It's one thing for him to leave my bed without so much as a note, not to mention the fact that he hasn't even sent me a text message or email since then; not even so much as a thank you, although, I probably would have taken offense had he done so, but regardless, that isn't the point.

But for him to stand here, in front of me, acting so damn formal, as though our night together meant nothing to him, just pisses me off.

His lips turn up at the corners, a smile itching to break free, and it only increases my anger, my blood now boiling at an all-time high. With my balled fist at my side, I lean close to him again before speaking, "You think you can just fuck me and then pretend we are strangers the next time you see me?" I demand, my voice stern enough to make my point, but low enough not to draw any unnecessary attention.

"Whoa, there… I think you have this all wrong."

Damn fucking straight. I should be kicking the shit out of you, not wasting my time talking to you! You… prick!

BLAKE

An incoming text from Jaxon annoys me. Apparently, my sub for the evening arrived AT her home fifteen minutes after Jaxon arrived to pick her up. He then had to wait around downstairs as she got herself ready, putting Jaxon behind schedule.

Tardiness is one thing that grates on my nerves. I will have to reprimand her for her blatant disregard of both my instructions and my time.

I've been trying my best to look forward to meeting this Chantal woman. Her picture and the short conversation we had made it clear to me that she was a very petite woman.

She isn't my usual type, which usually runs to curvy brunettes, but I want something different tonight. I need to cleanse my palette of Alyson once and for all.

Alyson.

The enduring thorn in my side. A sweet, alluring thorn, which has sunk deep within my flesh. No matter how much I try to dig her out from where she's taken root, she only seems to dig in more deeply.

"Mr. Hanson."

I turn to find Jaxon striding purposefully toward me, a stern, annoyed look on his usually expressionless face.

Fuck. Chantal must be one hell of a handful.

"Jaxon, thank you. I will inform you when we're through."

Judging by the state of the woman standing behind Jaxon, that won't be too long from now.

She's wearing a green camisole and tight jeans that are cuffed at the ankle, exposing her silver ankle bracelet and a small butterfly tattoo. She keeps her head low, a clear indicator that she is no newbie to this lifestyle, but the stench of alcohol wafting from her lips is not lost on me.

Drunk. She's fucking drunk. And she has ignored instructions on what to wear for our evening. Jeans! She's fucking wearing jeans.

The venomous look on my face is not lost on Jaxon and he promptly shakes his head, silently agreeing that I have made a huge error in picking this woman.

"If I may, sir," he says, as he leans in closer, so as not to allow the blonde woman to hear him. "Judging by the rather lengthy phone call I overheard Ms. Addison have in the car, she recently lost her job. Apparently, she went out to blow off some steam before she remembered anything about her plans with you for this evening," he whispers.

I understand what he's was trying to do. He wants me to show this woman a little mercy for her insubordination but anger surges within me at the sight of her flushed cheeks, her nervous twitch, and the god-awful smell of cheap beer emanating from herm, which is all I can focus on.

"How fucking dare you?"

Both Jaxon and I turn instantly at the shrieking scream we can hear coming from across the room, but our view is obstructed by the patrons of the club who are gyrating away on the dance floor. I can't see the source of the screaming from where I am standing, but that voice seems eerily familiar.

When I hear no more screaming, I dismiss this distraction. Having Chantal to deal with, I turn to her. Her head has remained low, and she is nervously shifting from one foot to the other.

She should be nervous after the stunt she pulled tonight, I think to myself, as I eye her suspiciously.

Jaxon turns away with a brisk nod of his head, leaving me to address the very drunk Chantal.

"Come."

Striding towards the elevator, I don't bother turning to see if she's following along behind me. Being as experienced as she is, she must know that her actions tonight have angered me.

Maybe the little wench has had that in mind all along.

It certainly isn't the first time a sub has disobeyed my orders in hope of earning a little punishment.

Stepping inside the elevator, I don't bother to address her, keeping my eyes fixed firmly in front of me as she takes her place to my right, standing two steps behind me.

When the elevator sounds our arrival, I proceed to the door of my suite, with Chantal wobbling behind me at an annoying leisurely pace.

"Inside. Bedroom. Clothes off. Kneel in front of the bed," I demand, as I open the door.

ALYSON

"Look, Ms. Lane. I really think you need to calm down. You're causing a scene."

Fuck if I care! Let them see! Let them all see!

"How fucking dare you?" I shriek, as I slowly amble toward him, watching as he eyes me cautiously with each step I take. "What makes you think that you can just fuck me and then pretend that you don't know me?" I growl through gritted teeth, my voice laced with venom.

In my entire life, I've never been made to feel as cheap and as worthless as he is making me feel tonight. I know that he only wanted one night with me, but I never expected this, having him to treat me like a common hooker.

You shouldn't have come back here. Who do you think you're kidding? You aren't a sub. Fuck, you only had your first orgasm a week ago.

"I didn't…I mean…I'm not him," he groans, his eyes wide with trepidation. Drawing a breath, he continues, "I'm not Blake, Ms. Lane, I'm Derrick."

What the?

I jerk at his words, unsure whether or not I've heard him correctly over the erotic sounds of the music playing in the background.

Derrick?

"What are you talking about?"

Derrick lowers his hands, and it's then that I realize he had raised them in a gesture of surrender, possibly right after I screamed at him. He runs his hand through his hair, and for the first time, I notice the difference.

His hair is shorter and has streaks of amber running through it. His nose is straighter, but his jaw is a bit more rounded than Blake's square one. His skin is also smooth like Blake's, but it's a shade lighter.

Stunned, I gasp, as he slowly shakes his head.

"You see it now, don't you?" he chuckles, and I instantly want to die of embarrassment.

Fuck me sideways. He has a twin.

"But…you looked…I mean…how was I to… I'm sorry," I stutter, as I stand before him, silently wishing that the floor beneath my feet would open up and swallow me whole.

I've just embarrassed myself in front of Blake's brother. How the hell am I going to explain this? And why the heck am I so upset? Blake isn't some random boyfriend who I have any kind of claim on. He was just…what exactly?

Blake is an amazing fuck, who has you so hooked that you're acting like an addict.

I push the thought out of my head. My behavior has been completely irrational since I first met Blake. Showing up at the club, wearing these tight dresses in the hope that I might get a rise out of him and for what? What has it gotten me?

Tears pool at the corners of my eyes; the reality of how far off-center I've been this past week twists at my insides. This isn't me. It's never been me.

"Hey," Derrick whispers, as he slowly cups my face within the palm of his hand. "Don't sweat it. You're not the first woman to damn near assault me, mistaking me for my brother," he teases, trying to calm the crazy woman who just attacked him verbally.

I smile despite myself, not wanting to further this awkward moment.

"Let's get you a drink and a chair," he offers softly, his hand leaving my face to wrap around one of my shoulders.

Still unable to say a word, I mindlessly follow him, not sure whether or not I should just bolt from this place. The exhibits, the grinding, the sensual music coming over the speakers, all seem to amplify the reality that I've been ignoring since my first night at the club, since my first night with him.

It was your only night, Lane.

Inwardly rolling my eyes at myself, I take the chair that Derrick offers me when we reach a table in one of the more secluded sections of the bar.

"So, what are we drinking? Beer, wine or hard liquor?"

I raise my eyes from the dark wooden table, but my words are still stuck in my parched throat. He stares at me, awaiting my response and when that doesn't happen, he rises to his feet and saunters off.

"Hard liquor it is," he mumbles under his breath, as he leaves and it's only then that I release the breath I didn't even realize that I've been holding.

What the hell am I doing?

BLAKE

Chantal ambles into the bedroom after briefly looking around, no doubt in search of said bedroom. I didn't even bother to point her in the right direction, my mind instead preoccupied, as she peers into each room along the hallway, without uttering a single word. No rebuttal, no sighing, not a sound, as would any true sub. It's apparent that she is indeed an authentic submissive, despite her blatant disregard of my instructions about her attire and my order that she be ready on time.

She isn't any different than most of the women I've brought to my suite, and yet I can't help but feel tension in the air as I saunter over to bar to pour myself a glass of scotch. Her presence in my suite annoys me, although I can't understand why it would. Yes, she disobeyed a direct order, but in reality, this should excite me rather than annoy me.

I need to exert my control over her, punish her for her actions, and normally, just the thought of doing so would excite me, but not tonight, not since fucking Alyson.

What the fuck is Alyson doing to me?

She isn't even at the club, and yet her presence lingers, both downstairs and in my suite. It almost feels wrong to bring another woman to my suite, and I simply cannot wrap my mind around it at all.

Taking a large swig of my freshly poured drink, I feel the burn of it as it travels down my throat. Remembering Chantal, I finish my drink and place the glass down before heading over to the bedroom.

Time to forget Alyson once and for all.

"I understand that you've had a rough night," I say to Chantal, the second I enter the room, not bothering to look over at her as she kneels at the foot of my bed. Instead, I slowly unbutton the cuffs of my linen shirt, making my way to the chest that holds my necessary tools.

Opening it, I remove the first thing I find, a paddle, and, feeling completely uninspired, I move to stand behind her. Her head is bent low, and her hands are clasped behind her back, as she sits back on her heels.

"My instructions were clear, were they not?" I ask, my voice devoid of any emotion, as I peer down at her petite frame.

"Permission to speak, Sir?" she says softly, her breathlessness revealing both her desire and her acknowledgement of my detachment.

Has this been her plan all along?

"Permission granted," I grunt in response, eager to hear her speak, although I know that regardless of what she has to say, it won't matter much to me. Nothing she says, short of her safe word, will change what is about to happen here tonight.

"Sir, I apologize for disobeying you, Sir. I understand that I must be punished for my behavior."

She doesn't explain further and I roll my eyes, mostly at myself, for expecting anything more from this woman.

What the hell is wrong with me?

"Stand up."

She does as she is told, eagerly rising to her feet, expectantly awaiting her punishment; but as she stands before me with her head bowed down, her breasts perked high, and her nipples elongated by her excitement, all I can picture is Alyson.

"Fuck!" I groan loudly, before again running my free hand through my hair. Chantal, startled by my outburst, quickly glances up at me, her brows raised in confusion, and I can't help but feel that this is wrong, totally fucking wrong.

I need to leave. She needs to leave.

Dropping the paddle to the floor, I make quick work of rolling down my sleeves before quickly heading to the door. Just as I cross the threshold, it occurs to me that Chantal is still waiting for my instructions. Turning my head slightly, I address her, "Put your clothes back on. Jaxon will take you home."

Leaving the suite, I release a sigh of relief before strutting back to the elevator. Pushing the call button, I take my cell phone out of my pocket and shoot off a quick message to Jaxon. He will no doubt collect Chantal and return her to her home, although I know he will also wonder why our scene ended so soon. He won't ever question me about it, respecting our professional relationship, yet he will indeed wonder, nonetheless.

When the elevator sounds its arrival, I march inside, eager to leave the club. Just as the elevator doors swing shut, the image of not one, not two, but three women come to mind, and in that instant I want to pry the doors back open and escape.

The image of those the women, different in so many ways, but yet the same, two of whom I no longer have and the third one—Alyson, my most recent conquest, the uncanny resemblance they share...

Shit, shit, shit!

When I reach the main floor, I make a beeline for the door, eager to fill my lungs with the cool autumn air outside. My breathing is erratic, my palms are sweaty and suddenly the images all come flooding back to me.

Elizabeth.

The proposal.

The pregnancy.

The hospital.

The funeral.

That last image isn't of the time I spent hating the world. It isn't filled with my endless need to control everything around me since I lost Elizabeth and our premature daughter, both of whom were taken from me before I even had a chance to even begin my life with them. No, it's not about the pain and the unrelenting anger I felt toward Elizabeth for leaving me.

Alyson...

She is the final image.

ALYSON

Derrick soon returns with our drinks, and I greedily down mine in a matter of seconds. I know it's totally unladylike behavior, but at the moment I can't find it in myself to give a damn. Tonight was rough, really rough, and I need something to take the edge off.

The atmosphere is alive with tension as we sit opposite each other. It's damn near suffocating, even oppressive in here. Silence stretches like a taut rubber band between us, with neither of us saying a word, our eyes avoiding each other, as we each scan the room. The music is soft, almost soothing, and I watch as everyone on the dance floor puts Jennifer Gray and Patrick Swayze to shame with their dirty dancing.

"So, are you going to tell me what that was about?" Derrick asks, breaking the awkward silence between us.

His resemblance to Blake is truly creepy, but then again, they are twins. There are a few subtle differences, but they are not really noticeable until you take the time to carefully examine each of their facial features. Derrick's gaze is much less intense than I imagine Blake's might be if he were here staring at me, waiting for some explanation.

"I'm not sure," I answer honestly, my gaze dropping to study the glass in my hands.

I truly don't have words to explain my behavior earlier this evening, and what else can I possibly tell him? Will he believe that I mistook him for Blake, and that I was pissed-off because it seemed to me that he had used me and that our encounter meant absolutely nothing to him?

Yeah, that'll go over well. I'll look like a lovesick lunatic. I'm sticking with my original answer.

Derrick scrutinizes me intently, which I find completely unnerving, but somehow I manage to look back up at him and held his gaze.

Wanting desperately to change the subject, I decide to ask a few questions of my own. "So, are you a Dom, too?"

Two Hanson Doms. God help the women of New York.

Amused, Derrick snorts and a panty-melting smile appears on his handsome face. "Oh, God no. I'm not into any of that shit. I am an owner here, well, a silent partner. I play around from time to time, but I don't do any of that extra shit that Bla…" He suddenly stops in mid-sentence, his eyes moving over me with what? Pity? Empathy? I'm not really sure.

"You don't belong here, Alyson. That was obvious from the second I first saw you," he says softly, his eyes never leaving mine.

His concern for me is clearly evident. It appears that he thinks I am a weak, helpless woman who was somehow unwillingly dragged into his club and that I don't belong here. While I know he is correct in thinking that I don't fit in here at 'The Dungeon', for some reason, although it's still unclear to me, I want to be here. I want to throw caution to wind and actually do something reckless for once in my life. Isn't that the reason I agreed to meet Blake in the first place? A chance to do something new, something completely unsettling, without worrying about the repercussions?

"How do you know my name?" I ask, realizing that I never gave it to him; yet, there he sits, opposite me, seeming to think he has some kind of insight as to who I am, although I've not offered him any information about myself.

He grins, his eyes softening. "For starters, I make it my business to know everything about the members here, and two, a little birdie told me," he says simply. I blush, my cheeks turning pink, knowing that he's referring to Blake.

Blake, kissing and telling, I can't imagine.

"Oh."

"So, what do you do, Ms. Lane?"

I shrug my shoulders and roll my eyes, as I remember the mountain of financial problems awaiting me back at my apartment in the city. For a moment, I had forgotten the fact that if I didn't find gainful employment soon, I'll end up becoming homeless.

A soft chuckle escapes my lips when I realize that being in this alternate reality, 'The Dungeon', with Derrick and Blake, gives me what I need, or at least what I think I need, an escape, a temporary time-out from the problems that have been suffocating me. Here, in this sinful place, I can be whoever I choose to be, a mistress, a sub, a sex slave, although there is only one man I want to dominate me.

Blake.

When I am with him he opens something inside of me, and I desperately want to explore it further. I need to. I need this escape, but Blake only wants one night with me. He hasn't even made an appearance here tonight. Has he become sick of my stalker-like behavior, which I now realize is way beyond pathetic?

Releasing a sigh, I turn to face Derrick, "I just finished school. I have been looking for a job ever since, I graduated, and I can't seem to even get a damn interview," I respond, a little too honestly. My drink has obviously kicked in, making me much freer at divulging my personal information.

"A job, hmm," I detect a secretive gleam in Derrick's eyes.

"Yup. Allison Lane, jobless, hopeless, Dom-less. Quite the catch, don't you think?" I say, sarcastically, as I turn away from the table to face the dance floor.

I can still feel Derrick's gaze upon me, but I can no longer bring myself to look at him; instead, I stare into the crowd and watch the members of 'The Dungeon'. They all seem to be well-attuned to each other. They aren't exactly what I'd call normal. I mean, normal people don't generally frequent this sort of establishment, but they must know what they desire, know who they are, must know at least enough to allow themselves to freely explore their sexuality, uncaring of what others might think about their choices.

The atmosphere suddenly shifts, and all the hairs on my arm stand at attention, something I've learned to recognize during my last few times at the club and have come to refer to as, 'Blake-dar.' But, as I scan the room for him, my body now fully alert, I can't spot him anywhere.

Derrick notices the change in my behavior. He also turns to scan the room, but suddenly he rises from his chair and rounds the table to stand in front of me. "Care for a dance, Ms. Lane?"

Confused by his sudden mood-shift, I glare up at him, frowning, as I assess his smile and the look of kindness in his eyes.

"Um, sure, I guess. I thought that maybe Bla…" I start to say, but I quickly decide that it doesn't matter what I think. My Blake-dar is obviously not working, and there is no point in trying to let Derrick in on all the crazy thoughts running through my head. I've already succeeded in making myself look like a fool to him.

Taking his outstretched hand, I smile up at him and nod my head.

He isn't the Hanson brother I want to spend my night with, but I'm already here and I look damn good. I might as well try to enjoy the rest of the night.

It doesn't hurt that Derrick is fine as hell to look at.

BLAKE

I awake in the morning with a horrific headache, reminding me that I shouldn't drink in excess when I'm upset, but after my episode outside the club, a drink or ten seemed necessary at the time.

Clearly, I didn't think it though, since my head now feels as if it might explode.

By the time I arrive at work, the headache is a bit more tolerable, but it's still firmly pounding away at my right temple. My assistant, Ana, takes one look at me as I step off the elevator onto the company's main floor and she just shakes her head, her motherly scolding all too evident in her expression.

"Mr. Hanson," she greets me, her tone clipped, which makes me feel like a small child in her presence. Knowing precisely what she's thinking, I decide not to address her tone of voice, and instead I offer her a smile.

She glares up at me for a while before her lips eventually curve up into a small smile. I've just successfully avoided her lecture on the perils of drinking to drown out my problems. Several years ago, when I lost Elizabeth, my drinking to excess turned into a daily problem. Since then, I barely drink at all, only allowing myself one or two at the club when necessary, but last night I strayed very far from that rule.

Are there any rules anymore? I don't know. Looking back over the past week, I no longer seem to know my right from my left. From the moment Alyson first stepped into the club, she turned my world upside down, or did she do that from the very beginning, with her response to my ad? I can't be certain, but I do know that I need to steady this roiling cauldron of emotions that she's been stirring within me since that first night.

Strolling into my office, I find that Derrick is on time for once, and he's sitting at my desk with a shit-eating grin plastered on his face. Surprised, I raise an eyebrow for a second before frowning back at him.

"To what do I owe this?" I ask, gesturing at him with my hand.

Still grinning like a boy, he promptly rises to his feet and mutters, "Oh nothing, I just want to turn over a new leaf, that's all," he replies, all too knowingly, and I immediately scan the room in search of whatever...

I know that damn smirk. The shithead is up to something.

"I am in no mood for this shit, Derrick. I had a long night."

Nothing seems out of place, I realize, after briefly scanning my office, strolling over to my desk, brushing past my brother, and plopping down on the leather chair behind it, which is still piled with unfinished briefs.

"You look like shit… again. What the fuck, bro'? You look even worse than you did at the damn start of the week," Derrick announces, as he flops down onto one of the other two chairs placed in front of my desk.

"Yeah, yeah. Look, I need to get some of these briefs prepared before my one o'clock appointment, so if you're done doing whatever the fuck you were doing in here, you can leave now," I tell him, gesturing towards the door. "You can also do some actual work, since you've obviously decided to actually come in on time. That's an order!"

Snorting, Derrick stands up and ambles over to the door.

"Save the ordering around crap for your subs," he amusingly barks back at me from the doorway. I would normally scold him for bringing up my personal business at work, but I simply don't have the energy at the moment.

"Work! Go! Now!"

He opens the door and then glances back at me, "We have an interview today at nine for the legal secretary position. Try to fix yourself up for it, will ya?" With that, he leaves and I sag back against my chair at the sound of the door closing behind him.

This is going to be one hell of a day.

Well, there is at least one positive outcome from last night's events. One thing that became painfully obvious to me the second I awoke this morning, leaving my brutal headache aside.

I need to see Alyson. There is simply no other way to deal with the constant turmoil she's causing in my life, other than to see her again and deal with the emotions she's been dredging up. Since Elizabeth's death, I haven't allowed myself to think of her, not even once, ever mindful of to keep her and her betrayal behind me, in the past, where it belongs. It's the only way; the only path to take after suffering her loss and in the aftermath of her leaving me, and taking with her…

Sighing, I wonder how I could have so totally missed the obvious clues. Scrolling down through my email inbox, I pull up the photo that accompanied Alyson's resume, although it still isn't clear to me what I found so compelling about her at the time. Now, as I again stare at the beautiful woman in the image, I know what it is! Her dark, wavy hair, her soft, pink, pouty lips, and her eyes, her fucking eyes are breathtaking and they are all too familiar.

Elizabeth.

Alyson is the spitting image of her, and I didn't even realize the similarity between them until last night, but it is was all too clear to me now.

Queuing up a new message to her, I stare blankly at the screen as I try but fail to come up with the words I want to say.

Somehow, 'Feel like being tied up and spanked for torturing me?' just doesn't seem to work.

Soon, an entire hour has passed, and I still am unable to find the right words to express myself. Frustrated, I push away from the desk and groan aloud. It's taken me years to repair the damage Elizabeth caused. In the wake of her death, I was reduced to feeling like less of a man, little more than an empty shell, feeling nothing but pure agony every single second of each and every day. I have no interest in ever being that person again.

Perhaps, sending Alyson an email isn't the best course of action I can take. I will not allow any fucking woman to destroy me again.

Glancing at the time, I realize that I'm already late for the interview.

Great. Just fucking great.

Our secretary, Gina, will be gone for a least three months on maternity leave, so we are desperately in need of a fill-in, even though my personal assistant, Ana, has been doing her best to fulfill both roles as we interview prospective replacements.

Grabbing a legal pad and a pen, I strut out my office, grateful for a task that will at least keep my mind off Alyson, even if only for a few minutes.

ALYSON

Running my hands through my hair for the millionth time, I step into the elevator, thankful that it's empty. Standing in the farthest corner, I attempt to steady my speeding pulse.

What is it about the Hanson men that makes me so damn nervous?

The elevator chimes as it reaches the thirty-seventh floor, and jerks to a stop as the steel doors swing open, revealing a sleekly contemporary reception area.

An older woman, smartly dressed in a pinstriped black pantsuit, looks up from her modern glass desk and smiles as I approach her.

"Hello, welcome to Hanson & Hanson. How may I help you?" she cheerfully greets me.

I return her smile. "I have an appointment, no, I'm sorry, I mean I have an interview scheduled today at 9:00 a.m.," I say, haltingly, my reply sounding more like a question than a statement.

Get your act together, Lane!

The receptionist looks at me knowingly, and says,

"There's no need to be nervous, dear. Mr. Hanson informed me of your interview and he will be with you shortly. I'll show you to the conference room. I'm Ana, by the way. Mr. Hanson's personal assistant."

I sigh in relief as I return her smile. It's sweet of her to offer me a calming word and I'm grateful for her empathy.

She gestures for me to follow her and I do, reminding myself that although I have no experience working in a corporate office, I do have more than enough administrative experience.

Thank you Mrs. Robinson, for having me to do all the administrative work for your classes. It seems that I owe you one for being such a hard taskmaster during my internship.

Following Ana down the corridor, she opens the door to what I assume is the conference room, and we both enter.

The room is huge and there is a very large, rectangular, glass table dominating much of the floor space. Surrounding it are at least twelve black chairs. The entire span of the wall to the right of the table is taken up by floor to ceiling windows, which offer a breathtaking view of the city.

Drawn to the view, I slowly walk over to the windows, leaving the receptionist behind me at the door. I've never seen anything quite as breathtaking as the view before me. I feel as though I'm on top of the world.

"Mr. Hanson will be in shortly," she tells me. I somehow manage to pull my eyes away from the view long enough to offer her a grateful smile, although I want nothing more than to admire the beautiful skyline forever. "If you need anything, please come and find me."

"Thank you so much, Ana."

She then turns away, leaving me to admire the amazing Manhattan skyline. The view from my apartment is nothing compared to this. It's breathtaking and I almost immediately feel completely removed from my problems.

Last night was a real low point for me. My obsession with Blake has truly gotten out of hand, and my embarrassing encounter with Derrick proved it. Although Blake makes me feel things I've never felt before, I know I don't belong in his world. I know it and so does Derrick, which means that Blake probably feels the same way. I need to accept that my night with Blake, although amazing, was little more than a small blip in my life, something that I'll always appreciate and remember, but something that I'll have to move past. It's high time I stopped being so irresponsible and also about time I started to take care of the problems in my life.

Spending all that money on 'The Dungeon' was a major error in judgment on my part. I hope that this interview will help me rectify that.

"Beautiful isn't it?" I hear from behind me, and I smile as I continue to admire the panorama before me.

Derrick comes to stand beside me and also admires the view.

"I have never seen anything like it. This surely beats my downtown view," I chuckle.

"How did you know it was me?" He eyes me suspiciously as he gestures for me to take a seat at the conference table.

Rolling my eyes, I give him a playful swat of my hand, "I have my ways, despite my embarrassment last night. I guess I wasn't paying attention to the differences at the time. Anyway, this is your company. Why would I expect to see Blake here?" I query playfully as I take a seat next to him, setting my purse down on the desk.

He smiles as he leans back in his chair. "We should be starting the interview soon. I'm just waiting for one more person to arrive."

"Okay. I'll just get out my resume."

Shuffling through the contents of my large purse, I withdraw the manila folder that contains my resume, a generic cover letter, and my letters of reference, since I didn't have a chance to research the company beforehand. I'm ready, or at least as ready as I'll ever be. Derrick didn't tell me much about the company last night, only that he's a lawyer, and that his firm was in need of a secretary. After I repeatedly turned down his job offer, not waiting to take what seemed to me like handout or pity, he was persistent and pretty much steamrolled me into agreeing to this interview.

Taking a deep breath, I spread the documents out in front of me. I'm ready to convince both Derrick and whoever it is that we're waiting for, that I will be an amazing secretary, despite the fact that my experience is, for the most part, just in teaching and assisting.

The door opens, and I close my eyes to steady my nerves, but my stomach is churning. My skin prickles with goosebumps even though I'm wearing a blush pink blazer with my charcoal pencil skirt and it is fairly warm in the conference room.

Releasing the breath I've been holding as the door opens, I'm met with a familiar scent. My eyes spring wide open, only to find the last person I need to see today standing there.

You've got to be fucking kidding me!

BLAKE

"Ana, I am expecting a call from Joseph Adinolfe this morning. If he should call while I am in the interview, please transfer the call the conference room."

Ana nods at me. "Not a problem, Mr. Hanson."

I continue down the hall toward the conference room, my headache still slightly pounding on the right side of my head. I groaned inwardly at the realization that I should have taken an Advil before heading into the interview.

Coming to a stop at the conference room door, I take a deep breath and mentally prepare myself for the interview. Though Derrick and I have turned this company into a successful one, we still conduct all interviews personally, wanting to learn as much as we can about each and every prospective employee before hiring them. We know this isn't the traditional way to conduct business, but we like to assure ourselves that our employees are personally handpicked, making our staff feel more like a family.

Stepping into the room, I come to an abrupt stop, the breath suddenly knocked out of me, as I stare at the woman seated at the conference table with her eyes closed.

What the fuck!

My eyes shoot to Derrick, who is wearing a smug grin spread, as he leans back in his chair enjoying my reaction.

Fuck!

I return my attention to Alyson. Her eyes are now open wide and she appears both startled and confused as she stares back at me in horror. Clearly, she wasn't in on whatever plan my brother concocted, and I can't help but wonder when and where she met my brother to begin with.

Had she somehow mistaken him for me? Does she appear so to be so perturbed and confused because he duped her into believing that he was me? Surely, Derrick wouldn't have done that to her!

I watch her breathing accelerate, as her eyes dart from me to my evil brother, and before either Derrick or I can say anything, she jumps to her feet, rapidly stuffing her paperwork into her purse and marching toward me.

God, she looks so hot when she's angry.

"Alyson, wait!" my brother calls after her, as she pushes her way past me, not bothering to stop even though she bumps into me in passing.

Turning to Derrick, I glare at him. "What the hell did you think you were doing?"

"I just thought that if I could get the two of you together in the same room, then, well, maybe you might grow a pair and realize that you fucking like this girl," Derrick says, owning up to his scheme, and shrugging his shoulders.

In that moment, I know that I've never felt more anger toward him in my life, and although I want nothing more than to kick his fucking ass, I need to go and find Alyson.

Turning on my heel, I stride out of the conference room in search of her; she'll more than likely be waiting for the elevator by now. After taking only a few quick steps, I round the corner and find her kneeling on the floor. Her purse is on the floor beside her and both of her hands are cradling her face.

Shit! She's fucking crying. Great going, Derrick!

Unsure of what to say to her, I do the only thing I can think of.

Taking hold of her left hand, I pull her to her feet and without saying a word, I lead her away, relieved that she doesn't offer any resistance.

Ana, eyes us suspiciously as we pass the front desk and continue heading toward my office. Pulling her inside, I close the door behind us and lock it before twirling her around and doing the one thing I've been wanting to do since the second I first laid eyes on her in the conference room.

My lips capture hers in an instant, and my headache immediately disappears the moment I feel her plump lips touch mine. I pull her closer to me, wanting to eliminate the space between us. It's been too long since I last had her in my arms, and the feelings that overwhelm me as she parts her lips to give me access to her mouth, are completely foreign to me.

Soon, we are nothing but eager, hungry hands and exploring tongues, as our kiss deepens. She moans into my mouth, causing my now steel-hard cock to twitch inside my pants. Her fingers caress the hair at the nape of my neck, as one of my hands grips her thigh through the fabric of her skirt. My other hand caresses one of her ample breast, and I groan aloud. There are too many layers of clothing separating us from each other.

As I tug her jacket from her, she hurriedly pulls away from me, panting as she backs away.

"No. We can't do this," she whispers, with her eyes firmly closed as she tries but fails to regain her composure.

"We need to end this once and for all," I respond, in a firm tone.

ALYSON

Holy shit! I can't believe that I'm making out with Blake in his office. How hot is this?

When he first entered the conference room, a look of confusion etched all over his perfectly chiseled face, I knew that Derrick was playing a dirty trick on both of us. There was never a job interview in his plan. He tricked me into seeing Blake, even though I cannot, for the life of me, understand why he orchestrated this.

I became so upset that I stormed out of the conference room, but just as I rushed past Blake's stoic form, his enticing aroma assaulted my senses, instantly weakening my knees. I haven't stopped thinking of his uniquely masculine scent since that first night, but as I strode past him, I realized that the mere memory of him just wasn't enough. I miss him terribly, and it makes me feel completely vulnerable, which, in turn, makes me feel rather pathetic, since he's not made even one attempt to contact me since that night. I was certain that he thought I was stalking him when he first walked into the conference room to find me sitting beside his twin brother.

Collapsing to the floor as soon as I rounded the corner in the hall, I'm unprepared when Blake appears, reaches out, takes my hand, and leads me into his office. The second he closes the door, he leans down and kisses me, really kisses me. I fall against him, melting into his hungry embrace. It's almost as though he's been away at war and is just now returning home, the flames between us practically crackling in the sexually-charged air around us. I need him, and I can feel that he needs me too.

Then, as he struggles to free me from my jacket, I can feel my body suddenly fall from the cloud of arousal it's been on, right back down to reality. I know that I have to stop him, even though every part of me wants nothing more than to stay in this moment with him.

"This is all wrong. You must think I'm a stalker or something, showing up here like this, but I swear, to you that I had no idea…" I start to explain, but Blake cuts me off in mid-sentence.

"Alyson, I know that my brother is responsible for bringing you here, and I do not think you are a stalker," he says, as he slowly closes the space between us.

His jaw is tense, his eyes are fixated on me with a look of clear determination. "Let me deal with my brother," he begins, as he stops within inches of me, his hands coming to rest on either side of my hips. "Right now, all I want is to get reacquainted with this sexy body of yours. If memory serves me correctly, I am your Dom, and as your Dom, I don't take too kindly to being made to stop."

Fuck. Me. Sideways. Damn, that's fucking hot!

"Yes, Sir," I whimper, just before his lips recapture mine as his hands simultaneously make quick work of removing my skirt.

He groans as soon as his hands reach my bare skin, and I grin into his kiss, loving the fact that I had been completely vain this morning and worrying about panty-lines, I had carefully chosen from among the thongs I owned, before deciding on the one that I'd worn when I last visited 'The Dungeon'.

As Blake lifts me into his arms, I wrap my legs around his waist as he carries me to his desk, and gently sets me down on its cool wooden surface. He never breaks the kiss, not even as he rids himself of his suit pants and frees his cock from his boxers.

When he finally pulls away, I moan expectantly, wanting desperately to feel his hard fullness inside me. When I hear his sharp intake of breath, I look up to discover that he's admiring me with his hooded eyes.

"You are so fucking beautiful."

My heart rate quickens as I stare into his mesmerizing eyes. He begins to run his hand over my breast but then stops to unbutton the silk blouse I wore for the interview. Once done with that task, he cups my lace-covered breasts in each of his hands and firmly squeezes them, drawing another whimper from me.

This is so fucking intense.

"I'm going to turn you over now," he says, using his Dom voice. Place your feet on the floor as far apart as you can, and hold onto the desk as tightly as you can," he orders, and all I can do is nod in response.

As this point, I'll do anything he asks. I cannot remember ever being more turned on, and I want nothing more than to have him take me.

"Good girl," he praises me as I obey him,   grip the edge of the desk, and spread my legs wide apart for him, bending forward at the waist and resting my head against the cool surface of his desk.

"You've been a very bad girl, Alyson. Do you know that?" His hands caress the soft, fleshy cheeks of my ass, and I moan in response to his touch. The pressure within me builds with each passing second. His hands, his scent, his voice, and the fact that we are in his office, all contribute to increasing my deep need for him, a need that aches to be fulfilled by only him.

"You seem to have broken yet another rule. Just. One. Night," he says, as he bites into my flesh with each word, causing my already wet pussy to become drenched with desire.

"What shall I do to punish you?" he asks, his voice barely above a whisper against my sensitive skin, now covered with goosebumps where his warm breath brushes against my skin.

"Please…." I moan, as I push back against him, hoping for some kind of relief.

"Tell me, tell me what you think your punishment should be, Alyson. What do you think I should do?"

Groaning against the desk, I raise my hips and push myself back against him.

"Please, Sir. I need you."

"What do you need, Alyson?" he asks, as he stands behind me, his cock now teasingly positioned at the entrance to my hot core.

"Fuck me, Sir... Please, just fu..."

Suddenly, I am filled with one thrust of his hips and it feels sensational. Blake pulls back, almost leaving my body completely, and then he thrusts back into me with such brutal force that I almost lose my grip on the table.

Yes. Yes. This is what I want. This is what I need.

Without warning, Blake's hand connects sharply with my ass and I yelp in surprise.

"That's one. Count out your punishment, Alyson," he orders, right before he spanks me again, even harder this time.

Shit. That one stings.

"Two," I call out with a whimper.

Blake continues to thrust into me, hitting the perfect spot inside me each and every time. He doesn't slow down the speed of his thrust, as he brings his hand down, striking against my ass again and again. Soon the pain turns into to unbelievable pleasure. I am a panting mess, crying out my torturous pleasure as he pounds into me relentlessly, continuing to dole out my punishment.

The combination of pain and please is absolutely amazing, and the pressure within me steadily builds until I am sure I am going to combust. A final blow comes down against on my backside, just as I tip over the edge and begin to soar high in orgasm.

"Oh, God. Ten," I scream out my release, my breath coming out in short, staccato pants.

Blake doesn't let up, continuing to pound into me. His hands are now gripped tightly around my waist as he continues to pull me back to meet his body with each pounding thrust.

BLAKE

I just can't seem to get deep enough as I relentlessly pounding myself into Alyson. She is gripping my cock so tightly inside her, and she's so warm and sweet. I just can't seem to get enough of her.

The sweet sounds of her moans draw me in and make me want to fall to my knees to taste her on my tongue, but for the life of me, I can't bring myself to pull out of her long enough to do it. She feels too damn good and I need more.

Of all the women I've ever been with during the past three years, being with Alyson renders me awestricken. She is so fucking perfect.

"Yes. Oh, God, yes!" she cries, as I impale her from behind, hitting her sweet spot over and over again.

She tightens her grip on me, and I begin to feel the walls of her pussy trembling as another release draws near. Snaking one of my hands around her, I find her swollen clit and stroke that bundle of nerves as I continue to drill into her clenching, hot pussy.

Just as she falls over the cliff into her orgasm, she pushes her upper body off the desk, a loud gasp escaping her throat, as she comes over and over again and pulls me along with her as I come forcefully within her.

"Fuck," I groan, and fall against her as my release shoots into her hot depths.

We remain there, panting, as we both fight to control our breathing. Pulling out of her slowly, I kiss her neck.

"I've missed you," I whisper against her neck, but her body suddenly stiffens at my admission.

She pushes back against me and shoves me away from her, before she frantically begins to look for her clothing and begins to dress.

"You don't have to lie," she mutters, as she draws on her blazer and buttons her blouse.

I am completely caught off guard at her sudden mood swing.

"What are you talking about?" I ask her, as I slowly amble back toward her, but she raises her hands to stop me from getting too close.

"Stop! You don't have to lie to me. We both know this is a mistake. You made that perfectly clear when you never called me. I don't belong in your world, and you know what else? I finally realize that fact. So you and your fucking brother should just leave me the hell alone," she demands, as she picks up her purse and strides to the door.

"Alyson, you have it all wrong," I say, trying to persuade her not to leave, calling out to her as she unlocks the door and steps through it, but she is gone in an instant.

What the fuck?

AN EROTIC ROMANCE

JUST ONE *Night*

VOL. 3

ALYSON

I can still feel Blake's heated gaze, his soft caress, his smoldering kiss on my eager lips and it's driving me mad. Three days have gone by, and I can't help but feel a bit disappointed that he hasn't reached out to me. I can't blame him. I did, in fact, walk out on him after he gave me the best orgasm of my life.

There will never be another man like Blake. I am ruined. Ruined for all men because of him.

I miss him. I know that I shouldn't. I know that it's silly to miss someone I never truly had, but I can't seem to help it. Blake stirred my desires. He dusted off the cobwebs I had allowed to take up residence in those forgotten places and he quenched a need I didn't even realize I had before I met him. In another life, another time, I'd cross heaven and earth to be filled by him again, but I know that leaving him was and is for the best.

Blake and I are from completely different worlds. Yes, he seemed willing to let me explore this forbidden lifestyle with him back in his office, but we both knew the truth. I was not who or what he truly desired.

Had you been his top choice, he would have called, messaged, texted, emailed... something.

But he hadn't. Why? Because he'd asked for an experienced submissive and ended up getting a green impostor. The fact that he'd taken his time with me each time we'd been together further proves my point. He'd been holding back, keeping the beast within himself tame, because I am not suited for him. Plain and simple.

Had it all been just a joke to him? Let's seduce the inexperienced girl who answered the ad thinking she was responding to ad for a substitute teaching position and string her along just as you would a junkie on crack, just for the hell of it? It's cruel.

I'm sure that by now he's found a replacement, a woman who knows just what he needs and who gives him the control he desires. That's exactly what I want for him—to be free to be himself and to be happy in the life he has chosen, even if it means that I'll be living in celibacy, saving myself the embarrassment of having to tell whomever I may meet in the future that I've been ruined by a truly masterful lover, one who I couldn't have, but whom I still desire.

God, I am so pathetic! Just the thought of Blake with another woman makes me cringe.

Climbing into bed, I try to force all thoughts of Blake out of my head. I have bigger fish to fry and wasting time thinking about the man I want so desperately, but will never have, won't do me any good.

You still need to find a job before the end of the month or you'll be sleeping on a bench in Central Park. The thought makes me shudder.

Sighing, I pull the covers up to my chin and close my eyes. Tomorrow I will focus on finding work. Tonight, I'll dream of him, just as I have every night since I walked away from him.

BLAKE

It took a few days for me to calm down after what Alyson pulled. The rage I felt deep within me as I watched her walk away from my office was undeniably the angriest I've been since Elizabeth's death. *What is it about women that makes them think that they can just walk away from me?*

Alyson didn't realize it then, but she's made a big mistake. It's one thing to agree to go our separate ways, it's another to shoot me down and walk away after casting her evil spell on me. No, Alyson made the wrong choice, and I am going to make sure she knows it.

But first… "Stand up and walk over to the bench," I command.

Suzie, my latest conquest, eagerly jumps from her position across my lap and saunters over to the bench across the room. I watch as her reddened ass cheeks glide over to the padded wooden bench with a seductive sway, and as she knowingly kneels before it and awaits my next command.

The delicious sting in my palm from having spanked her pear-shaped ass is just an appetizer. I have big plans for Ms. Suzie, ones that I know she will thoroughly enjoy.

She doesn't look anything like Alyson. Her hair is cut short, and is a blue-black color. She's curvy, and her breasts are ample and perky. Yet, Suzie's body does absolutely nothing for me, unlike Alyson's body, which begged to be caressed. Suzie will still serve her purpose nonetheless, giving me a much needed distraction.

"Safe word?" I ask, in a controlled, clipped tone as I slowly advance toward her. I know her safe word, but I like to be sure to remind a sub to use it if need be. I may be a bit of a sadist and a dick sometimes, both of which I am absolutely okay with, but I am not one to take what is not freely given to me.

Suzie seems ready and willing to submit to my every command. From our email correspondence, I know that she is dominant in almost all aspects of her life. She was only introduced to this lifestyle one year ago, but I can tell that she is a natural at it. She's a free-spirited woman, but she is often misunderstood, at least, that is the impression she gave me. It almost seems to pain her conscience to submit to men, but I believe that every woman has a craving for domination. They want to be bent to someone's will, pushed beyond their boundaries, and told what to do. And while externally, Suzie may put up a tough front, I can read her like a book. I could see the desire building within in her the second she entered my suite. She wants to be thoroughly ravished. I, of course, wouldn't be the gentleman I am if I didn't give the little minx what she wants.

I made sure to have her sign and fax over the contract. Since Alyson, I've been diligent in getting the contracts in order and signed prior to meeting a new sub. I will not allow myself to be caught off guard again. Thankfully, Alyson isn't the kind of woman I need to worry about or I shudder to think what the repercussions might have been.

No, Alyson isn't avaricious. She has an innocence about her that is intriguing. That innocence, coupled with her dark desires, and her natural, instinctive responses to the pleasures of the lifestyle, make her truly special.

Now, standing behind Suzie, I notice that her cheeks are flushed with desire. Rosy pink hues cover her skin as she breathlessly responds, "Red, Sir."

As I bring my hand to the nape of her neck, she shudders beneath my touch. Her breathing quickens and her skin heats under my fingers. She wants this. Wants me. And, I suddenly feel like I am at home again.

It's been way too long.

Since meeting Alyson, I have definitely been off my game, blindsided by the emotions she evokes in me, but now, here in my suite with this woman. I am once again in my element. There is no confusion between us. There are no pesky emotions to contend with, other than the delight we'll share tonight and tonight alone. I need not worry about what she will do with herself once she is escorted out by Jaxon. Suzie is mine to do with as I see fit for the next few hours. My commands are what she yearns for. There are no questions, no turmoil, and no complications to overcome, because she freely surrenders herself to me knowing that I will make this experience memorable for her.

And that I will, indeed.

"On your feet," I command, letting my hands fall away from her.

She whimpers at the loss of contact, but readily does as she is told. "Yes, Sir," she says once she's standing.

"Kneel on the bench with your arms stretched wide and your legs spread apart," I order her, before turning away to retrieve the items I have already set out for tonight's encounter.

Eagerly, she's assumed the position on the bench. Her arm and legs are spread wide and her pear-shaped ass is in full view for me. Her pussy glistens with moisture and my mouth waters at the sight.

I approach her slowly, carrying my tray of instruments. Once I reach her, I set down the tray on the wooden table alongside the bench before picking up a bottle of lube. Pouring a generous amount into my hands, I kneel behind her, making sure not to touch her just yet.

I lean in until my breath softly caresses her ass. She whimpers. She grips the edges of the bench tightly, her knuckles turning white with strain, and I know that she's desperate to feel me on and against her.

"You like to be in control, don't you, Suzie?" My lips brush against her heated flesh ever so slowly as I ask my question.

She groans softly before answering me, "Yes, Sir. I have to be."

I quietly utter a tsk-tsk sound behind her, as I place my hands around the soft flesh of her ass. Gently, I massage the lube around her tender flesh, earning a moan from her lips.

"Do you wish to be in control now?" My right hand comes down sharply on her bottom just as she opens her plump, pink lips to respond.

She yelps out a "No, Sir," and I re-commence massaging her ass with my fingers.

"You're dripping," I say, as I softly graze my fingers through her silky folds. "Care to take a look?"

She turns her head toward me just as I bring my finger to my mouth and close my lips around it. Shuddering at the sight of me tasting her wetness, she is unprepared when I suddenly plunge two fingers inside her. She gasps in surprise and I expertly flick her clit with my thumb.

Drawing away from her, I stand up. I can hear that her breathing has changed to staccato panting as I walk to the left of her and buckle first her left hand and then her left leg securely to the bench. She watches me intently, wondering what I have in store for her as I do the same with her right hand and leg. She doesn't utter so much as a sound of protest and for some reason I am bothered by that.

I pick up the black silk blindfold I purchased earlier today. I groan inwardly that I felt it unsuitable to use my red one on any woman other than Alyson, but it seems as though her magical effect on me still lingers even after she's gone.

Pushing all thoughts of her out of my mind, I cover Suzie's eyes with the piece of black silk and secure it behind her head, successfully plunging her into darkness. She instantly tenses up, her instinct to bolt nearly boiling to the surface, but she calms quickly as I brush my hands over the curves of her body to quiet her nervousness.

"You want to give in, don't you Suzie? Even while your instincts tell you to take control, you want to offer me this, to give yourself to me freely, and let me do with you as I wish," I purr against her ear, as I slowly select the riding crop from the tray.

Suzie moans a response as I begin to trail the crop from the middle of her back down to her still reddened ass.

"Please…" she pleads, when I brush the crop against her heated pussy, coating it with her dripping wetness.

Swiftly, I pull the crop away from her, "Ah, but we mustn't get ahead of ourselves. We have all night to play," I tease, as I quickly tap the riding crop against her swollen nether lips.

A shrieking scream bursts from her lips at the sudden sharp contact, but all too quickly she thrashes and pulls against her restraints, "More. Please, Sir. I need more," she pleads.

As you wish.

ALYSON

The hammering at the door pulls me out my delicious slumber and I groan in frustration as I climb out of bed. "Damn it, I just got to the best part of my dream," I mumble to myself.

Glancing at the alarm clock, I wonder who in their right mind would be pounding on my door at six-thirty in the morning. Grabbing my soft, plush robe, I quickly throw it on and tie it before sauntering to the door with a yawn. Not even bothering to look through the peephole, I open the door wide while in mid-yawn, with my eyes still closed.

"Did you really just open your fucking door without looking?"

My eyes spring open instantly and my breath hitches.

What the hell?

"No, asshole. Normally I don't have to worry about people coming over at freaking six in the morning. Had I known it was you, I would have stayed in bed!" I bark back at Derrick, hating the small smirk he's sporting.

The nerve of him!

After everything he's done, he has some nerve showing up here. He practically served me up to his brother on a silver platter to get my heart broken.

"Calm down, will you," he says, as he brushes past me, entering uninvited despite my obvious lack of enthusiasm at seeing him.

Letting the door slam closed, I whirl around and march straight up to him. "What the hell are you doing here?"

The last thing I need in my life is another reminder of Blake. It's bad enough that I have to give him up, but having his look-alike show up at my apartment just won't do. I need him to get the hell out of here as soon as possible so that I can at least try to move on.

Yeah, like that's really gonna happen, Lane.

I shake my head at the thought, and give Derrick the evil eye. He holds my angry gaze for a moment before finally relenting and wrenching himself away from me. Unwelcome though he may be, he turns around, ambles over to the couch and takes a seat in my living room, patting the seat beside him. "I need to talk to you."

I can't believe how arrogant Derrick is, not that he doesn't have a reason to be. He's gorgeous and he knows it, and that is a dangerous combination. Not for me, of course, because he is not the Hanson brother I want, but he's certainly a threat to the rest of the female population. Derrick is a lethal weapon that should be kept under governmental surveillance. I'm sure most women would be falling all over themselves at the mere thought of him showing up at their door, in much the same way as I'd fallen all over myself when Blake showed up the night I met him. Derrick just grates on my nerves.

So much for getting to the best part of my dream.

"So," I begin, standing directly across from Derrick, "To what do I owe this honor?" I cross my arms over my chest and glare at him.

When he realizes that I am not going to make this easy for him, he sighs, runs his hand through his hair and takes a deep breath. "Look, I am sorry about what happened. I thought for sure if I got you two in the same room you guys would work things out, but apparently I never considered the possibility that you'd run out on Blake. Had I known, I would have stayed out of it. Do you have any idea what being on Blake's shit list is like?" he grumbles, his exasperation evident.

I try to keep from smiling at the thought, but fail. I just know that Blake is probably putting Derrick through hell, and rightfully so. "It serves you right," I chuckle, as I let my defensive stance slip. "You have no idea what I wanted to do to you that day. Castration was very high on my list," I jest, loving the horrified look on Derrick's face.

"You wouldn't dare!" he mock gasps, cupping his package protectively.

I shrug my shoulders and take a seat across from him. "No, I probably wouldn't. I am not as cruel as you might think. But, try that again and I swear that whatever Blake has done to you to pay you back will be a walk in the freaking park compared to what I'll do to you."

Derrick's lips curl up into a tight smile, and he nods his head in agreement, "Noted."

Silence descends on us momentarily, and I can't help but feel a bit awkward, sitting across from him wearing nothing but my robe, while he's dressed in a perfectly tailored, charcoal grey suit.

The Hanson brothers sure know how to wear a suit.

Clearing my throat, and reining in my drifting thoughts, I ask him to give me a few minutes to get dressed. Derrick nods his head and I quickly return to my bedroom, closing the door behind me.

The second sexiest man ever to walk into this apartment and here I am in a fucking bathrobe—not that I had any plans to sleep with him. But, still... how embarrassing.

I grab a pair of yoga pants and a light blue tank top and quickly change. Running to the bathroom, I make quick work of brushing my teeth and taming my unruly case of bed head.

Deciding that I've done the best I can with my appearance, I march out the bathroom and back into the living room where I'd left Derrick. "So," I begin to say, but I trail off when I realize he's no longer there. Turning on my heels, I can't help but gawk as I see Derrick's large frame moving around my kitchen and scrambling eggs.

I was so not expecting that.

"What are you doing?" I ask, finally gaining his attention.

He turns and smiles at me before returning his attention to the eggs he's preparing. "I figured that since I woke you up, the least I could do was to make you breakfast. Consider it a peace offering," he replies, as he carries the now well beaten eggs over to the frying pan. I don't buy this act, not one bit. Something is definitely amiss.

"Okay, that's it! Step away from the frying pan, buddy," I demand, my right hand taking up residence on my hip.

Surprised, Derrick drops the spatula he's holding and turns to face me. I eye him suspiciously as I slowly approach him. "I don't know what the heck you're planning, but you can forget about it. I am not buying this act of yours, so spill it. You can start with how the hell you knew where I lived."

Derrick smirks, clearly unfazed by my outburst, as he simply grabs a chair from the kitchen island and plants his ass down onto it. "You are one smart woman, Alyson. It's no wonder my brother is so smitten by you," he laughs.

Narrowing my eyes, I take the bait he offers, "Smitten? Your brother doesn't do *smitten* and you and I both know it. So what exactly is this about?"

Cocking his head to one side, Derrick gives me a shit-eating grin, and I know instantly that I am not going to like what he has to say.

"I have a plan. A good plan actually. But, this time I am bringing you in on it," he says, as he leans over the island.

Oh, great. Derrick has a plan. Because the first one went sooo perfectly. This man is nuts.

BLAKE

Suzie was an excellent distraction for me last night, but there is a certain troublesome little problem named Alyson that I need to deal with, and sooner, rather than later. Alyson will understand that I am not a man to be so easily turned from, and I plan on making that fact very clear to her.

The first part of my plan is already in motion. The moving company I sent over to her apartment this morning should have packed up all of Alyson's belongings by now. Glancing at the clock on my desk, I wonder why I haven't heard from the little witch yet. Surely she will have quite a lot to say to me once she realizes that not only is she not walking away from me, but that I am moving her into one of my condos.

It's obvious that Alyson has misgivings about her ability to adapt to a D/s relationship. Although I initially had no interest in training a sub, I can't deny that the idea of training Alyson arouses me. Training a sub is no easy task. It's a lot of hard work for both the Dom and sub, which is why I have avoided it for so long. She doesn't have to live there permanently of course, just until her training has been completed. In the meantime, she'll want for nothing. I'll make sure that her apartment is taken care of and that she has everything she needs while she's at the condo.

I know she'll be a raging ball of fury when I see her later. I must admit that I am looking forward to it. She is absolutely captivating when she is riled up, which is exactly the way I want her.

"Jaxon, please check with the movers and make sure that our guest is prepared for me," I tell him, as I enter my home office to find him standing beside my grand oak desk.

"Sir, I have just spoken to the movers, and it seems we have a bit of a situation," Jaxon murmurs, clearly uncomfortable about whatever he has to tell me.

Raising an eyebrow, I signal for him to continue as I take a seat behind my desk.

Clearing his throat, he continues, "It seems that the movers have not yet had the opportunity to procure Ms. Lane's belongings."

Straightening up in my seat, my brows draw close together into a frown. "What do you mean they haven't done it? Isn't that what I am paying them for?" I bark at him, my impatience evident.

Jaxon shakes his head, but pauses before continuing, "It's your brother, Sir. He was at Ms. Lane's residence when they arrived and apparently he ordered the movers to leave. They were very confused as to why you would hire them only to send them away before they'd had a chance to fulfill their obligations."

Jaxon took a giant step backward, just as I picked up the Bey-Berk antique brass bull statue that was on my desk. Without another thought,

I threw the priceless piece of art across the room, letting it hit the wall, as a blast of red-hot fury surges through my veins.

"What the hell was my brother doing at her house?" I fume, as I rise from my seat and round my desk.

Jaxon doesn't cower as I approach him, instead he straightens his back and looks me in the eyes. There is no doubt that he could probably kick my ass if I step too far out of line with him, but right now I just don't give a damn. I want answers and I want them now.

"That is a question you will need to ask your brother, Sir. I called him shortly after I spoke to the moving company. He is expecting your call, but says that he will be in attendance tonight at The Dungeon should you wish to speak to him face to face, although I seriously advise you against it."

Glaring daggers at my assistant, I take several deep breaths in an attempt to calm myself down. I am not one to lose control so easily.

"Let my brother know that I'll meet him at the club, Jaxon. Have the car ready to go at eight sharp." I tear my gaze away from his steely appraisal. If the man has an ounce of nervousness in him, I can't tell. That is something that I usually like about him, but today it just seems to further aggravate me.

"As you wish, Sir," he responds, as he turns away to leave me standing alone in the middle of my office.

Just before he reaches the door, he turns his head back toward me, "For the record, Sir. You'd lose," he says, as he chuckles softly. "It seems that Ms. Lane arouses great passion within you. I surely hope that you are worthy of her."

With that, he turns and walks out of the office, closing the door behind him.

ALYSON

This is a stupid idea.

Derrick spent the entire afternoon explaining all things BDSM to me, and now I can confidently say that I am an expert on the subject. At least on paper I am. I obviously haven't yet had the chance to put any of the things he's gone over with me to use.

According to Derrick, Blake needs a little push in the right direction. He is convinced that I am absolutely perfect for his twin brother, even though I have been adamantly opposed to his theory. Blake and I are worlds apart, and even after I explained that to Derrick, he brushed it off as inconsequential.

It was then that he decided to bring me up to speed on all things D/s. He was very thorough and he even pulled up several websites as exhibits, and drew several diagrams. I didn't have any idea that Derrick was so kinky, but apparently he is worse than his brother. He did make sure to let me know that he only uses his gifts on his girlfriend for the most part.

Lucky gal.

It's been a nonstop cramming session since early this morning, with only a brief, and I mean very brief pause, when Derrick suddenly needed to retrieve something from his car. When he returned, he seemed a bit on edge. I wanted to ask him about his odd behavior, but decided against it. It's more than likely he was just nervous about the possibility of his plan backfiring.

Oh, and it is surely going to backfire, Lane, I think to myself, as I step into the dress Derrick handed me after his return from downstairs. I didn't have a chance to examine the beauty of it while Derrick was here. It's a breathtakingly stunning, gold-accented, crystal-embroidered, single-shouldered teal dress in silk crepe. Its hemline reaches a little above mid-thigh and it hugs me in all the right places. It appears that Derrick has amazing taste in women's clothing.

If only he was gay. I have been meaning to find a gay male friend. Maybe he's bi?

Chuckling to myself, I release the curls I'd pinned up in my hair before I took my shower, and allow my dark tresses to fall freely into soft waves. My makeup is simple and elegant, shimmery, gold glossed lipstick and golden eyeshadow that helps accentuate my eyes.

Stepping into a strappy, gold high-heeled sandal, I feel like a million bucks. Giving myself a once over in the mirror, I still can't help but wonder why I agreed to go along with Derrick's crazy plan.

I know how it's going to end. Nothing good will come of this, and yet, for some reason, a small part of me can't help but hope that his plan will work. Who knows? Maybe Blake wants this as much as I do.

Don't hold your breath, Lane. He's more than likely going to be furious with you.

Sighing, I turn away from the mirror and pick up my purse. It's too late to back out now, and I know that if I skip out on this plan of Derrick's, he'll only come up with another crazier one. For some reason this has become a very personal mission for him.

Straightening my shoulders to project an air of confidence I don't really feel, I walk slowly to the waiting car service vehicle that Derrick sent over. Climbing in, I try to calm my growing nerves.

The driver, a young African American man, rounds the car after seating me and peels off the second he's back behind the wheel. This is very much like my first ride to The Dungeon, and I am beside myself with worry.

What if he doesn't take the bait? What if he couldn't care less? What if he has another woman with him? That final thought causes bile to rise in my throat, but I quickly swallow it down. *Why, oh why, did I agree to this?*

By the time we reach the Brooklyn Bridge, I am hunched over, with my head between my legs and breathing deeply. The driver looks over at me several times during the ride with a puzzled look on his face.

"Uh, Miss? You all right?" he asks for the tenth time, and I lift my head up slightly and give him a silent thumbs up.

Am I all right? Fuck no, I am not all right, but telling him that won't help me one bit.

I can do this. I can do this, I tell myself repeatedly, but I know that I am quickly losing it. Another thought crosses my mind just as we finally navigate off the bridge and I truly fear that I am going to throw up.

God, this plan is totally dependent on Blake stepping in and stopping us, but what if... Oh, God. I can't do this!

BLAKE

Jaxon drops me off directly in front of The Dungeon and I don't bother waiting for him to open my car door. We barely said a word to each other during the entire trip, for which I am grateful, given the fact that I had allowed my emotions to get the best of me right in front of him.

"Shall I accompany you, Sir?" Jaxon asks, once I exit the car, with my back to him.

I turn toward him and regard him intently. Jaxon is my best employee. We've always managed to keep our relationship strictly professional, although right now his disapproving eyes look more fatherly than I would like. I suppose he views me as a father would view his son, since he is several years my senior, but I need neither a friend nor a parent in this relationship.

"No. I will call you when I need you to return," I curtly reply, as I watch his jaw clench tensely at that remark.

When he doesn't respond, I turn to the entrance of The Dungeon, ready to get to the bottom of my brother's business with Alyson.

"Sir," Jaxon calls out to me, just as I make it halfway to the door. I release a deep sigh as I turn around to face him, and simply say, "Jaxon."

He clears his throat and releases a breath before walking toward me. Standing just a few feet away, he looks me directly in the eyes. "Sir, I mean no disrespect, but please tread lightly with Ms. Alyson," he says. He squares his shoulders and faces me, obviously anticipating a negative response as my brow furrows.

"Excuse me?" The volume of my question doesn't seem to faze him as he continues to stare at me. Jaxon has never stepped this far out of line in the three years he's worked for me. His forwardness is completely out of character, and it almost makes me want to cut him some slack. Almost.

"Sir, I have known you for three years, and, after the sudden departure of your..."

I don't let him finish, "Be very careful, Jaxon. I am your employer and I would suggest that you remember that. My personal affairs are no concern of yours," I remind him.

"Very well, Sir," he sighs, and he shakes his head before turning away and getting back into the car.

By the time he drives off, I am fuming mad and the urge to hit something is intense, but I will myself to calm down. Losing my temper before I meet with my brother will do me no good. I need to keep a clear head or this night will end very badly... for him.

Striding to the entrance of The Dungeon, I head to the elevator with purpose. Derrick has a lot of explaining to do. I can't for the life of me justify any reason he might have had to visit Alyson at her home, and certainly not alone.

Has he been visiting her daily ever since she stormed out of my office? Were they now seeing each other?

Endless questions swarm my mind as the elevator sounds its arrival. Stepping inside, I try to remind myself that Derrick is my brother, my identical twin brother. He is many things—cocky, troublesome, and irritating—but he is not one to take what doesn't belong to him.

And Alyson belongs to me!

Exiting the elevator, I take a deep, calming breath before trekking down the long hallway that leads to the door of The Dungeon's main floor. Once I've steadied my emotions, I continue to make my way down the long dark hallway and open the door.

You'd better have one hell of an explanation, brother.

ALYSON

The dimly lit room does nothing to calm my nerves. I can't help but feel anxious. There's a full house here tonight at The Dungeon, and the exhibits have more onlookers than usual.

Derrick is already here when I arrive, and has set everything up for our planned ruse. He tries to reassure me that his plan will work, but, of course, I hear none of it. The only thing I hear is the pounding of my heart inside my chest.

Pulling me up onto the slightly raised platform, Derrick leads me to stand in front of a reinforced, freestanding St. Andrews Cross at its center. He's already informed the appropriate managers of the slight change of plans in this evening's entertainment, and it is now time for us to begin. My eyes scan the club, searching for any sign of Blake, but, to my disappointment, I don't find him.

"Are you sure he's coming?" I ask Derrick softly, as I stand directly in front of the Cross, a sea of onlookers staring up at me.

"Absolutely," he whispers back, discreetly, before he backs away from me to permit the spectators to get a better view.

My breath hitches in my throat as I take in the number of people expectantly gaping at us. Unlike the other exhibits lining the outermost walls, Derrick had managed to get us a center platform, thus allowing viewers to completely surround us. The center platform is normally reserved for special guest. That's what Derrick told me when I first arrived. Since Derrick is one of the partners, it was easy for him to arrange for us to be center stage.

You can't do this. What are you thinking, Lane?"

Derrick loosens his royal blue necktie and undoes the top two buttons of his crisp white linen shirt. He looks almost as handsome as Blake standing there to my right.

I gulp, and I drop my purse to the floor of the platform, and mentally try to prepare myself for what is about to happen next. Derrick promised me that he would be my guide through this, but I just can't shake my nerves. My clammy hands are shaking as I turn my eyes away from him and briefly close them.

Well, it's too late to back out now, Lane. Just try to just pretend that it's Blake who is doing this to you.

Opening my eyes once again, I try to dial down my anxiety level, and steel myself for this final game. *If only I knew for certain that Blake will really show up here tonight to see this, I might be better able to ready myself.* But, there is no way to know for sure that he'll be watching, and Derrick's confidence does nothing to reassure me. He was so sure that his first plan to trick Blake and me would succeed, who's to say that this plan will turn out any better than the last one.

He walks across the platform, his sleeves now rolled up to show his strong, solid forearms. "Follow everything I tell you to do. No questions, no hesitations. We have only one shot at this. It needs to seem real," he murmurs softly for me alone to hear.

Nodding my head ever so slightly, I await his first command.

"Take off your clothes. Leave on the heels," he instructs, just before he again steps away from me.

Heat rushes to my face, but I do as I am told. Slowly, I unzip my dress and allow the soft material to fall away, pooling at my ankles. Stepping out of it, I stand up straight, wearing nothing but my barely there lace lingerie. Not knowing what to do with my hands, I let them fall to my sides.

The music changes to a slow seductive beat and I can't help but close my eyes and allow it to take over, my body slowly swaying from side to side.

Yes, I can do this, I tell myself, as I lose myself to the sensual beat.

Derrick's soft breath tickles my shoulder, "You are so beautiful. Do you know just how fucking breathtaking you look right now?" He doesn't whisper this. He says it loud enough for the watchers to hear. To my surprise, and I am sure, to his, I moan in response and immediately tense up the second I hear myself do so. My hands come up to cover my breasts, but my eyes remain closed, unwilling to face our audience just yet.

"No, don't shy away from me, my sweet," he cajoles into my ear, as he gently lulls me into calmness, his hands now softly caressing my arms.

"That's it, darling. Let me guide you. Don't fight it," he instructs me, and, to my surprise, I find myself relaxing into him, letting go of all my uneasiness.

Derrick takes hold of my right hand and brings it up over my head. He fastens it to the cross behind me with the attached straps, and then does the same with my left hand. I feel him kneel down in front of me. His hair tickles my legs as he pushes my legs wide apart, and then straps them down to the base of the cross as well. He tugs at the restraints, checking to make sure that they are secure before stepping back, no doubt letting the onlookers take me in. He seems to enjoy giving them a show.

"Look at me," he dictates, and my eyes fly open to find that he has removed his shirt. I can't help but gape at the sight of him. Just like Blake, Derrick's body is virtually flawless. The sexy dips and grooves around his abs makes me instinctively lick my lips.

What the hell are you doing, Lane? Stop ogling Derrick! I chastise myself, and force my eyes to look away from his hard, chiseled chest and his all too lickable abs. Raising my eyes up to his face, I see that Derrick is smirking knowingly. He's clearly caught me gaping at him.

Yeah, somehow I don't think he's bisexual. He's totally hetero. So much for finding my new gay bff.

Derrick strolls over to a nearby table and picks up a flogger. He turns back to face me with a mischievous glint in his eyes. My eyes widen as he slowly ambles closer, his moves both unhurried and strong.

What is he going to do? I wonder, but, in truth, I know just what he's about to do to me. I've seen the videos, watched as Doms flogged their subs deliciously until they were squirming and begging for more. I want nothing more than to experience this with Blake, but, being center-stage in The Dungeon, just a few feet away from Derrick as he approaches me with the flogger in hand makes me panic.

A sheen of sweat coats my body as I wait for him to proceed. My eyes again scan the room in search of Blake, but I still don't see him.

Derrick stops directly in front of me, blocking my view of the crowd. His hands come up to grip my hair firmly. He tugs it back and his gaze falls to my lips. My chest rises and falls in anticipation, but he doesn't attempt to kiss me.

Instead, he brings the flogger up to my shoulder, softly letting it caress my body. Slowly he moves it over my breasts, first the right one and then the left, and my rapid breathing intensifies. Then, suddenly and without warning, he cracks it against my right nipple. Hard. The pain shoots through me. I yelp and then cannot help but moan at the sweetness of the pleasure that surfaces in the wake of the pain. Liquid gathers in my panties, and I hate my body for reacting this way, but I know it believes it's in the hands of its Master—my body associating the delicious pain with Blake, even though it's Derrick who stands before me.

This is so wrong. Blake, where the hell are you?

BLAKE

Walking into The Dungeon, I head straight to the bar. I am very much in need of a stiff drink before my meeting with Derrick. Between Jaxon's sudden interest in my personal affairs and my brother's secret appearance at Alyson's home, I feel as though I am losing control and I cannot allow that to happen.

I have spent a long time developing a system in my life, making sure that everything goes accordingly. However, in the past few weeks everything about my system seems to be unraveling, especially ever since my first conversation with Alyson.

She is the reason for it all, and I know I should walk away from the enchanting woman, but I can't do that just yet. We have too much unfinished business.

The bartender, the same collared young man who served me during my first night with Alyson, places a shot in front of me as soon as I reach the bar. He gives me a knowing look, then smirks slightly and walks away. I throw the shot back and wince. It's strong, just the way I like it.

I slam the glass down on the bar, and close my eyes. Taking in a deep breath, I feel the burn of the amber liquid as it works its way down my throat.

Nice.

"Another," I yell back at him, and he nods.

Glancing at my watch, I realize that Derrick should already be here, but I don't bother turning around and scanning the crowd for him. He knows where to find me.

The collared man slides another drink in front of me and I immediately throw this one back too. I don't wince this time, but I feel the burn of it as it travels down my throat as I place the now empty glass down on the marble-topped bar.

My eyes close for just a second and that's when I hear it.

That sound. God, I've missed that sound.

I don't open my eyes just yet, instead I try to focus on the sounds in the room. My hands twitch when I hear it again, and I spin my stool around and begin to scan the room.

Has that vixen decided to play with my mind again tonight? I wonder, remembering how she'd visited me on the nights following our initial meeting.

I look at each exhibit, my eyes first scanning along the outer walls looking for the curves of her body, the cascading softness of her hair, and her temptress eyes, but I don't see her. Normally, she'd visit each exhibit, looking at whatever piqued her interest and then she'd move on if she found herself bored. She'd feel my eyes on her and then disappear into thin air just as our eyes first meet. It's always the same, and yet also somehow different each time.

I hear it again. A soft moan pierces the slow rhythm of the music, and I crane my neck to look deeper into the crowd. I know she's here, just like before, but for some reason she isn't making herself known.

The Dungeon is packed tonight, with most of its patrons gathered at the center of the room, which is odd since the center stage exhibit is only used for special occasions.

I'm too far away, and at the wrong angle to see which guests occupy the stage, so I push myself off the stool. Wending my way through the sea of mingled hands, grinding bodies and soft, guttural murmurs, I make my way to the front of the center stage.

Is that the cracking of a whip? A flogger? I'm not sure, but the sound of it striking naked flesh vibrates through the air, emanating from the stage set before an audience of at least one hundred people.

And then I hear it again. It's her.

So soft a sound, yet deafening to my ears, it freezes me just a few feet away.

There's a St. Andrew's Cross before me, and I stop dead in my tracks with only one thought in my head.

Mine.

Alyson.

ALYSON

Holy shit. That hurts!

My clit throbs deliciously in the wake of Derrick's assault, but I can't focus on it. I can't enjoy the burn or the pleasure that flogger gives me as Derrick again cracks that freaking flogger against my core.

Where is he?

Is he coming?

Fuck, that really hurt.

Why do I like it so much?

Is this what Blake has been holding back from me?

I am distracted. My mind races, even as Derrick wields that fucking beautiful flogger against me again and again.

I cry out in sweet agony, scorching pleasure and worry. I feel my body's reaction to his assault trickling down my legs.

God, this is so wrong! Lane, what the fuck are you doing?

I am panicking, my heart is racing, my breathing is erratic, yet still Derrick doesn't yield. Grabbing my hair with one of his strong hands, he pulls it to the side, exposing my neck to him and he lowers his head. The scents of his soap and woodsy cologne tease my nose and I can't help but tense up when he licks the base of my throat.

He shouldn't be the one doing this to me.

I close my eyes and repeat these words over and over to myself.

Pretend it's Blake. Pretend it's Blake. Pretend it's Blake.

Derrick bites down hard on my shoulder. I scream, long and loud even as he laps up the stinging sensation with his tongue.

Fuck.

Tears stream down my face, but I can do nothing to wipe them away. My hands are still tied down and I can barely move them an inch in their restraints.

Derrick doesn't let up. His tongue moves across my shoulder to my collarbone. I shudder at the feel of it and I fear that he truly believes I want this from him. My body is betraying me.

I do want this, but not with him. He's what's wrong in this erotic scene. I've dreamed of this countless times since meeting Blake and it's always beautiful, and so incredibly erotic. But, Derrick... he doesn't belong here in this scene with me.

Why the hell did I ever agree to this?

Fear still grips me and I am quivering against him by the time Derrick rises.

Blake isn't coming. I've made a terrible mistake and I now fear that Derrick may have lied to me all along.

He stops, brings his mouth to my ear and whispers softly, "It's show time."

And then I feel it.

The hairs on my arms stand at attention, my nipples become engorged into sharp peaks and the electric charge in the room suddenly shifts. I should feel relieved. I should feel joyful that he's arrived before Derrick and I took things too far, but I feel none of that.

Only one emotion courses through me, even as Derrick is suddenly yanked away from me by brute force and punched in the face.

There is one feeling I can't run away from. Looking at the square, rigid set of Blake's jaw, his scolding gaze and his fisted hands, it feels as though a heavy weight has been laid upon my chest. It's so heavy, and I want so badly to push it off of me, but I know I can't, neither physically nor mentally.

One look at Blake's hard, clenched jaw proves that what I am feeling is not irrational at all. His dark, primal scrutiny of me now affirms the feeling within me and even amplifies it.

I'm scared.

Shit. What the fuck did you do, Lane?

So much emotion flashes through his beautiful grey eyes, but one emotion is far more prominent than the rest.

Anger.

"Blake," I whisper softly, my eyes imploring him to understand. I have never before seen such ferocity in Blake's eyes. His gaze bores into me, ignoring the disappointed sounds of the viewers who were enjoying the scene. Blake doesn't care at all whether or not they want the scene to continue.

It feels as though the room and its occupants fall away in that moment and it's just the two of us, and I'm now the sole the focus of all his anger.

Should I bother explaining?

Will Derrick explain on my behalf?

The sound of Derrick groaning somewhere to the left of me momentarily draws my attention away from Blake. Hunched over and cradling his face, Derrick manages to glance my way and I feel horrible that he's hurting.

A beautiful, petite woman walks up behind him and crouches down. She pulls him to her, gives him a kiss, then looks up at me and winks.

Ah. His girlfriend. Lucky gal.

Had this entire situation not become so fucked up I might have laughed, but there is nothing remotely funny about it right now.

When Blake steps forward, close enough to block my view of Derrick and his girlfriend, my breath hitches. Without saying a word, he unties my hands, first the left and then the right. I awkwardly bring them down, rubbing my wrists where the bindings cut into my flesh. As Blake then bends down to release my feet from their restraints, I don't move a muscle. Even after he's done freeing me, I'm not sure what I should do.

When he picks up my dress and places it in my hands, I want to think that he understands what Derrick and I were up to, but the look in his eyes as I take back my dress is cold and vacant of emotion.

"Blake," I begin to attempt an explanation, but, in that instant his lips crash down on mine in a bruising, scorching kiss. His hands grip my hair and cradle my neck, and we're nothing but tongues and teeth at the moment. This kiss feels different. It's not romantic in any way. It's almost desperate, both pleading and fucking hot at the same time. I can feel his anger as his hands drift down from my hair and he begins to tug, pull and squeeze the flesh of my hips, thighs and ass.

He grunts into my mouth as my tongue explores him. My mouth is begging in the only way it can, at this moment, for him to understand what's going on, but his caress is punishing, unyielding and purely animalistic.

He then pushes away from me, leaving me reeling from our kiss. "Blake, it's not what you think," I start to say, but his darkened eyes arrest me into silence. He doesn't smile. Doesn't say a word. His breaths are now coming out in short pants, filled with drunken lust.

I want to pull him close, kiss him again and make him see that I only want him, but he doesn't give me a chance. Before I contemplate uttering a single word, he turns and stalks away, the onlookers parting like the Red Sea as he leaves me there, alone on the platform, both confused and deeply ashamed. I can only stare after him, his strides unhurried, yet strong and powerful.

"Go," Derrick manages to grunt at me, and I can see that his beautiful face is already bruising. "Upstairs. Now."

Blinking a few times, it is only then that I grasp what Derrick is telling me and I quickly pull on my dress. I don't even answer him. Instead, I leap off the platform and push past the gawking patrons.

I have to explain. He needs to understand.

"Blake! Wait!" I call after him, but he doesn't slow or turn to face me. His hands are balled into tight fists by the time I reach him and grab his arm.

"Please," is all I manage to say, but Blake brushes me off. He doesn't look at me as he steps into the elevator, nor does he even turn around to face me once he's inside. Instead, he keeps his back to me even as the doors close behind him.

What have I done?

BLAKE

Fuck!

It's completely insane, I know that, but even though she's practically whored herself out to my brother just to make me jealous, I can't deny that seeing her up there—panting, moaning and taking all the punishment that my brother meted out to her turned me on.

She isn't as fragile as she seems.

Still, I am furious with her and Derrick. It didn't take me long to figure out what game they'd been playing up on that stage. One look at the expression on her face as I manhandled Derrick, told me everything I need to know.

The duality of her emotions was evident. She loved every bit of what Derrick did to her, but she didn't want to enjoy it quite as much as she actually did. I don't know if her uncertainties were because it was been Derrick up there with her instead of me, or if it was the public nature of the act itself. Nonetheless, it had been a trick all along. That much is clear. They wanted to get my attention.

They'd succeeded.

"Please," Alyson begs when she reaches me, gasping and tugging on my arm. Her touch, though deceptively gentle, is electric, and I can't allow myself to fall under her spell. I brush her off and step into the elevator. I knew she would run after me, and as she stands there behind me, imploring me to listen to her, I formulate a plan of my own. She'll soon see that I am not a man to be toyed with, not a man to be made a fool of, but that lesson won't happen tonight.

If she wants to play games, then play them we shall, but I will be the one pulling the strings and making the rules.

The elevator chimes its arrival at the lobby and I quickly shoot off a text to Jaxon. Luckily for me, Jaxon always stays close by.

Five minutes later, he pulls up in front of The Dungeon with a knowing look on his face. I don't engage him, even as I climb inside and pull the door closed. Nothing has gone right today and I am too pissed off to go back and forth with the old man now.

Flashes of Alyson up on that stage play over and over again in my mind, and try as I might, I can't stop my dick from twitching at the thought. Concurrent images of Alyson on my spanking bench with her soft, plump, ass in the air while I brand her butt red with my trustee flogger cause me to groan aloud. The need to bend her over my lap and spank her soundly for allowing another man to touch what only belongs to me is strong. I want to fuck her hard and fast. I want to punish her for her behavior tonight until she is writhing beneath me, but I need to do it right.

Now that I know that she is interested in taking whatever this is between us even further, I can plan my next move.

As far as Derrick is concerned, he will regret meddling in my business. I will never let it slide that he laid so much as one finger on someone who belongs to me. She may not know it yet, especially after I walked away from her tonight, but Alyson is mine. And I don't share what's mine with anyone.

ALYSON

No, go back to sleep, I order myself as I toss and turn in my bed, willing the morning to go away. Groaning, I pull my pillow from under my head and pull it over my face to try to muffle the banging sounds in my head. No such luck.

I don't even remember coming home last night, but somehow I'd managed to get here and climb into bed fully dressed. I can feel the dress now bunched up around my hips and my shoes are still on my feet. It was a very long and trying night indeed.

He walked away.

I completely blew it with Blake last night. There is no way he will ever forgive me—not that I'll even attempt to try to gain his forgiveness. After what I did, well, really after what Derrick and I did, there is no way I can ever face Blake again. At least Derrick shares his DNA, he'll get a chance to apologize and make up with his brother. Me? I am screwed. It's just as well.

Last night's events sealed it for me. I have to get over Blake. Somewhere between my fifth and ninth drink, I made up my mind. We are not meant to be together. The sooner I accept it, the better everyone will be.

I reluctantly push aside the pillow and crawl out of bed. The pounding in my head isn't going to go away on its own. I might as well get up and start my search for work.

Work. I need to find a job soon or I'll end up sleeping on the streets.

Darn hangover! I curse as I kick off my shoes and wince at the sound of the thud each one makes as it hits the floor.

Ambling to the bathroom, I barely recognize myself in the mirror. My makeup is smeared, my hair is a tangled, mangled mess. My eyes are glazed over and bagged underneath. I look like hell.

Well, what did you expect to look like after drinking all night?

I shrug at my reflection and then roll my eyes. Turning, I quickly turn the water on in the shower and rid myself of last night's clothes.

Hopefully, I'll feel better after a nice, long, hot shower.

***

Thirty minutes later I feel a little better, but the pounding in my head continues, although now it's more of a light thumping than the full hammering it was earlier. I pull on an oversized sweatshirt and underwear and plod my way to the kitchen, my hands cradling my aching head. A healthy dose of caffeine is what I need right now.

I am never drinking again, I silently vow, even though I know that I have no real intention to keep that promise to myself.

"You're up."

I stop, startled, and gasp aloud in surprise, clutching my chest as my heart beats frantically.

"Shit. I'm sorry, Alyson. I didn't mean to scare you, I swear," Derrick says, putting down the mug he'd been holding and walking towards me. "You okay?" he asks.

"No," I rasp, still trying to calm my breathing. "What the hell are you doing here?"

He doesn't answer. Instead, he reaches over to the counter and hands me my own miracle in a mug, coffee. "Just making sure you're all right, duh!" He grins his sexy, dangerous, grin and I can only smile and shake my head at him.

"Actually, I was just making you some breakfast. So off you go. Back to bed young lady," he shoos me away with a flick of his hand.

I'm not going to argue with him, not when whatever he's cooking smells so good.

Climbing back into my bed, I contemplate calling Blake, but really, what could I possibly say to him? 'I'm sorry,' just doesn't seem to be enough. I've never seen him so upset and who could really blame him? If the situation had been reversed and it was me who'd walked in and found him up on that stage, I'd be livid too. So, of course he's angry.

There is definitely no undoing or unseeing that.

"Here you go," Derrick says, as he enters my bedroom carrying a breakfast tray.

I smile and take the tray from him, my mouth watering at the sight of eggs, bacon, toast and what the heck is that?

"Grits. They're good. Eat up," he says, reading my mind and the look on my face.

"Okay. Thanks, for everything. I'm sorry I got you punched in the face." His eye was now a deep shade of purple compared to the bright red it had been last night.

"Ah, it's nothing. I've been through worse," he murmurs, as he takes a seat on the edge of the bed.

I want to ask him if he's spoken to Blake since last night, but I can't bring myself to ask. I bite down on my lips as I push the food on my plate around with my fork, feeling lost.

"He's not answering my calls," Derrick offers and I only give him a weak smile. "Look, I'm sorry my plan didn't work. I probably should have just stayed out of it. It's just…" he trails off, turning away from me.

"It's just what?" I encourage, wanting him to finish his thought. I'm not going to lie and pretend I haven't wondered why Derrick seemed so insistent that Blake and I get together. It's obvious that he cares for his brother, sure, but there has to be more to it than that.

"Nothing…" He's just been through a lot these past few years. He deserves to be happy."

After I finish eating my breakfast, Derrick takes my plate and heads out. He promises me that he will call and check up on me later and I mumble something incoherent as I snuggle back into bed. As I drift off to sleep, all I can think about is what Derrick said.

What hardship could Blake have gone through that would cause his brother to worry about him so much?

BLAKE

"You want to explain to me what the fuck you were thinking?" I practically growl at Derrick the second he steps off the elevator.

Derrick sighs and brushes past me, heading directly to my office without responding. He stops in front of my desk, and I close the door behind me before sitting down at my desk.

"You keep blowing it," he finally says to me, as if that is supposed to answer all of my questions.

"What the hell are you talking about?" I grunt, irritated.

He looks me in the eyes, his jaw tightly clenched, and says slowly and clearly, "You. Keep. Fucking. It. Up." He accentuates each word. "Don't you see that Alyson wants you just as fucking badly as you want her? Why the hell else would she have agreed to go down to The Dungeon and allow me to do all those things to her?" he spits out.

Wrong move.

The thought of all the things he'd done to her sends a fresh wave of anger coursing through me, and before I can stop myself, I am up, out of my chair, and grabbing him by the throat. "You should never have touched her," I hiss, my face only a few inches away from his.

Derrick pushes me away, breaking my hold, "What the fuck does it even matter, man? You walked away. You left her there crying and drinking herself into a pitiful state. Shit, I had to stay with her just to make sure she got home okay," he barks back at me, his hands balled into fists at his sides.

The strong urge to punch him in the face again is tempting, but his words finally penetrate my anger. "How bad?" I ask, needing to know that Alyson is okay.

"She'll live, no thanks to you," he snarls, as he takes a seat in front of my desk and props his foot up on the edge.

Groaning, I return to my own seat across from him. Silence falls over us for a moment. This isn't the first time Derrick has stuck his nose where it doesn't belong. In fact, he's been doing things like this during our entire lives, and even more frequently after Elizabeth's passing.

In truth, I wouldn't have made it through that ordeal had it not been for his meddling in my business three years ago. It was because of him that I joined The Dungeon and later bought into it as a partner. While I know that he's always had the best intentions, it hasn't stopped me from wanting to punch him in the throat from time to time—today being one of those times.

"She's not Elizabeth, you know," Derrick says suddenly. "I know you see the resemblance, but she's not her. Alyson's here, she's real, and damn it brother, she really likes you."

The resemblance between Alyson and Elizabeth is truly remarkable.

Having any version of Elizabeth near me again has two very different effects on me. While I want nothing more than to hold Alyson close and never allow her to leave me again, a possessiveness I never felt when Elizabeth was alive, but which I now find myself experiencing with Alyson. The other emotion I feel, clearly unrelated to how I felt about Elizabeth, is an uncontrollable deep, dark desire for her, and that is purely an Alyson thing. Something about the dual parts of her personality makes her unique when compared to Elizabeth.

While Elizabeth was very outgoing, she wasn't much into experimenting in the bedroom, not that I was particularly adventurous either back when we were together. But Alyson, she's a conundrum, an unexpected anomaly. Everything about her screams innocence, to the point where she'll adamantly insist one day that she doesn't belong in my world, and yet the next day where do I find her? Dead fucking center-stage at The Dungeon, scening with Derrick. Nipples erect, her breath coming in quick pants with her cheeks tinged pink with lust.

No, Alyson isn't Elizabeth. She is something more.

"Can she handle it?" I ask, knowing that Derrick will understand just what I am asking, what I need to know.

He nods his head slowly, his lips curling up at the sides, "Oh, she can handle it all right. That girl is tailor-made for you."

Taking a deep, steadying breath, I nod my head in agreement, "All right, well, since you will be my personal slave for the next three months as payback for doing what you did last night, I need you to do something for me."

Derrick groans, his shoulders slouching in defeat, "Damn it, what do I have to do now?"

It's time for me to claim what's mine.

ALYSON

It's dark and cool in here. The silence around me is almost deafening, but I forge ahead, clutching a note in my right hand, as I slowly feel my way around the room. I don't bother trying to read it again because it's imprinted on my mind.

I awoke this afternoon after a wonderful nap to find it slipped under my door. My initial thought was that Derrick had come by and left me a message, but as soon as I opened it, I knew it wasn't from Derrick.

'Your Master awaits.' That's all, just those three words and a time and location:

The Puck Penthouse. 9:00 pm SHARP! Dressed only in your evening coat and heels.

I have never been to The Puck, though I cannot imagine a single New Yorker who hasn't heard of the historical building. It contains six one-of-a-kind condominiums atop one of SoHo's most iconic buildings.

A combination of both eagerness and trepidation courses through me. Will he be angry with me? Does he plan to punish me for running away from him the way I did and for what Derrick and I did on stage at The Dungeon?

The thought of him exacting punishment on me should scare me to death, considering all that I've read about and watched regarding D/s relationships. I still can't help but clamp my thighs together at the thought of him, my sex greedy for all that he might have in store for me.

I've missed him terribly, and I know that it's been nothing but my pride that's kept me away from The Dungeon since that god-awful day I stormed out of his office. And, when I finally returned, with a nudge from his brother, Derrick, he still wasn't pleased.

I hear something shift, and I go still.

Is he here? Angry?

The pounding within my chest grows louder with each and every step I take, my chest heaving, my palms sweaty and the hairs on my arm…

I sense that he's here, watching, waiting…

Please come out, I silently beg him, but he doesn't. I can still feel him watching me.

I feel his heated gaze upon me, but I can't pinpoint his exact location, it's too dark in here. "Please," I whisper aloud, when it seems that he will not make his presence known. I turn around in place, trying, but failing to see even so much as an inch in front of me.

"Shh…."

Spinning around again, I only meet darkness at first, and I whimper in disappointment. I want him. I need to feel him against me. And, at that thought, as if he's read my mind, a curtain is drawn, allowing a floor of moonlight in just before I feel his solid, chiseled body press against my back not a second later. A shiver runs through me, causing me to gasp, and then to sigh in contentment.

"You've been a very bad girl," he purrs in my left ear, his hot breath teasing my earlobe, as my excitement at being near him again causes my pussy to glisten with heated moisture.

"Yes, Sir."

I lean back into him, enjoying the feel of his muscular chest against me, and it's only then that I realize that he's pulling my trench coat off my shoulders, knowing just what he'll find underneath. I am naked and exposed, exactly as he requested in the note.

"How shall I punish you?" he whispers, against my bare shoulder.

I shudder. It's been far too long since I felt his lips on me, felt his thick cock inside my body.

"Whatever you wish, Sir. I am yours to do with as you desire."

I need to make him see, make him realize. I want to please him, and show him that I've done my homework this time around.

Kneeling down onto the floor, I clasp my hands behind my back and bow my head. Blake's sharp intake of breath as I surrender myself to him makes me smile.

He is pleased.

"Rise to your feet."

Obeying his command, I stand up, but I don't turn to face him. Instead, I await further instructions, as my heart continues to throb with my need for him.

Suddenly, I feel his hands around my waist and he gently pushes me forward until I find myself against a wall. Swiftly turning me to face him, he slides his hands behind me and cups my bare ass, giving it a squeeze.

"Why did you come here, Alyson?" he asks, as he continues to massage my flesh, another moan escaping from my lips at his caress.

"I... I...," I try to speak, try to tell him how sorry I am and how much I have missed him, but the words lodge in my throat, and I am unable to speak.

"Nothing to say?" he questions, before lifting me up by my bottom, and placing my ass down onto a thick strap. "I guess I'll just have to fuck the answer out of you."

Before I can register what he is saying, he spreads my legs apart and straps each leg down at the thigh, so that my pussy is now fully exposed to him.

Blake steps away, and I begin to panic at the state of immobility in which he's left me. I wiggle my butt, trying to get some leverage, but it's hopeless.

"Stay still!" he demands, the sound of his voice coming somewhere across the room.

"Yes, Sir."

He makes a small tsking sound under his breath, and says, "Now you speak?"

He's angry. Fuck that. He is furious, and I am about to be punished, but for some reason, I am not afraid, even as I hear him slowly return to me and raise my hands into the air, where he uses another strap to secure them above my head.

I suddenly remember the red-haired woman at The Dungeon and how Blake caught me admiring their scene.

He remembers, I smile.

He steps away to admire his work, looking at me as I hang suspended in mid-air, with my pussy pushed forward and open to him, ready for him to do whatever he pleases.

"Your safe word?"

I've already given this matter some thought. "Lost," I answer him, knowing that it's the only word to explain how I feel without him. He's uncovered something inside me, and without him in my life, I have been completely and utterly lost.

"So be it."

At that, he slams his cock inside me, and I feel instantly sated, as though I've just returned home after years of wandering aimlessly.

I am home and home is with him.

BLAKE

"Blake... I..." Alyson stammers breathlessly, but a quick bite on her nipple distracts her from whatever she was planning to say.

I practically growl as I ease in and out of her, relishing the feel of her warm, tight pussy enveloping my dick with each stroke.

Fuck, she feels amazing!

Whispery moans slip out of her mouth as I pick up my pace, driving deep inside her which each thrust. I feel her begin to pulse from the inside out and I slow my pace to a crawl.

She whimpers in disappointment, but I don't speed up my movements. "No coming until I tell you to," I half growl, half moan.

Her eyes are tightly closed, her body is fully open to me. She's so fucking perfect, it's as if she was made just for me. Rolling my hips against hers, I am pounding into her with controlled force.

Breathing heavily, I crush my lips to hers, thrusting my tongue into her more than willing mouth. I can't explain the feeling that courses through me at the meeting of our lips. The need to have more of her pierces my heart. I need more, I want more. I can't breathe. My lungs tighten and I feel as though the air is being sucked out of me as I bury my head in the crook of her neck and inhale deeply. Her body surrounds me. Her scent is so sweet it makes my mouth water. The taste of her minted lips, addicts me, and her hot, slippery pussy draws me in and greedily swallows up and clenches around my cock.

"Why did you come here tonight, Alyson?" I ask, and I realize soon after the question leaves my lips that I've been asking her this same question from the very first night we met.

For some reason I am inextricably drawn to Alyson, as though there's an undeniable force pulling me to her even when I know I should run far away from her. I can't explain it, can't understand it, but here I am trying to get even closer as I bury my cock into her delicious, hot pussy.

Fuck.

"I need you," she cries out. I can feel the truth of her words as I continue my assault on her tight, wet cunt, loving the feeling of being deep inside her. Each time I slam into her dripping heat, Alyson's cries modulate up an octave.

Her pussy's grip on me tightens, and between her words and the feel of her around me, something within me seems to break. She's quivering and shaking against me and struggling against the restraints holding her in place.

"Come for me, Alyson," I growl, hammering into her with brutal force and her sheath immediately begins to pulse around my cock.

"Oh, Blake! God, oh God," she cries out, as she gives into her release.

I don't let up. I continue to pound into her, prolonging her pleasure and triggering my own. A guttural growl tears from my throat as I come hard, and she milks me clean. We're both panting, completely spent from the force of our orgasms, but I am far from through.

Alyson's words trigger something inside of me that I haven't felt in years. The need to make love to this beautiful woman is strong. And, as I slide my cock out of her, I feel the loss of her already.

What have you done to me, Alyson?

ALYSON

Blake unfastens the straps holding me up once our breathing evens out. His arms wrap around my waist as he holds me tightly against his strong, solid body and I shiver, trying desperately to prevent the tears I feel welling up in my eyes from escaping.

Blake severs our connection way too soon. He doesn't say a word to me as he turns on his heels and disappears. It's still too dark in his condo, but my eyes seem to have adjusted to the darkness.

As if on cue, the lights flicker on and I wince from the sudden intrusion. It takes a minute for me to realize that I'm in an empty room. A living room perhaps? I wonder where he's gone, but I don't wander off looking for him.

The room he's left me standing in is twice the size of my own living room. The floors are of wide oak planks. Contemporary chandeliers hang overhead, giving off a soft warm light. The walls are deep grey and bare, with wide, stark white moldings. Dark plum linen curtains line the walls, and I can only assume that the space behind them is practically wall-to-wall windows. The room is beautiful, even though it's bare of furniture. I sigh as I run my hands over the linen curtains, confirming that they feel as soft to the touch as they appear.

I didn't think I would ever set foot in Blake's suite again, especially not after I made a big show of storming out of his office a few days ago. Yet here I am, in this surprisingly normal looking room, and I feel a yearning to be in his suite again. All I can think about is how much I want him to order me to his bed as he did that first night.

Blake doesn't say a word to me when he returns to the room and I don't know if I should be happy or terrified about that. From the second I stepped into his suite tonight my stomach has been in knots. I want to explain everything to him, but what can I say?

That you walked out of his office and regretted it the second you did? That you would do anything to have him back? That you also regret going along with Derrick's plan?

It's true. I want to say all those things, and make him believe me. I need to show him how much he means to me. I want to give what Blake and I have between us a chance, but that's the problem.

What exactly is it that we have between us?

A part of me wants to just come right out and ask him, but another part, the part that sees that Blake is now in full Dom mode, knows that asking him to discuss what he witnessed last night would be foolish. And trying to get him to define our relationship so soon after my little exhibition last night is just plain crazy.

When did my life get so complicated?

Just a few short weeks ago I was a normal woman, a college graduate seeking employment. One misunderstood advertisement seems to have tossed me into this cluster-fuck of a mess.

I close my eyes and think about everything I have been through. Being the only survivor of the accident that killed my parents has deeply affected me for the past five years, more so because they'd not been around for any of the major life events your parents should be part of. Graduating high school, starting college, they missed it all. I'd received some psychotherapy, of course, but no amount of therapy can fully fix the part of me that broke on that day. I kept to myself after losing them, wanting to spare myself the pain of getting close to people again, only to have them leave me too.

It's a silly notion, I know. My parents didn't voluntarily leave me, but the loss hurts just the same. Even now, fifteen years later, I still keep myself closed off. I don't have friends. I barely had a love life before Blake. To make matters worse, my heart seems to be fixated on a man who is just as confused as I am, although he doesn't seem too confused tonight. No, he's completely in control and fuck-me-sideways, I love it!

I open my eyes to find Blake's hooded, lustful grey eyes fixed on me. My breath hitches at the sight of him standing in the doorway, leaning against the frame. His beautiful, sexy lips beg to be kissed. I want to lick my way across his strong jawline.

His penetrating eyes bore into mine and I feel my body moisten under his gaze. Just that look has me panting with need. He's wearing only a pair of low cut jeans, and he's barefoot. Just the image of me running my tongue along the dips and swells of his abs and pecs causes me to lick my lips in anticipation.

"On your knees, Alyson," he orders, as he allows his eyes to slowly caress every inch of me.

Swallowing hard, I want to comply. Really, I do. But I know that we should probably discuss what happened last night before going any further. "Blake, I really think we should talk..."

He doesn't let me finish. "No talking, Alyson. On. Your. Damn. Knees." His voice is rough and stern but still laced with lust.

I want to express my outrage, yell and scream that he can't order me around or speak to me this way, but the throbbing heat spreading through me causes me to moan instead.

How can he turn me on so much?

He doesn't want to talk right now, and I can admit to myself that neither do I, but still I hesitate. I ask myself for the first time in years if I am ready to let go of the hurt that's been burning in my heart. Am I capable of allowing this man to get close to me without fear and without knowing what might happen tomorrow, even if what tomorrow brings is nothing but turmoil?

Just the few weeks I have spent with him have already been the most thrilling of my life.

I know what my answer is. I think I have known it since that very first night.

Slowly I sink to my knees, my eyes never leaving his. I don't lower my head. Instead, I arch my back, giving him a view of my hardened nipples. Holding his heated gaze, I slowly bring my hands behind my back.

This is what you do to me, Blake.

Blake groans softly, and the sound registers between my legs. Jolts of electric current fire through me and I clamp my thighs together to keep from swooning.

I want to touch him when he approaches and stands directly in front of me. I want to feel the weight of his thick, sexy cock on my tongue, but I force myself to do only what he says from this point on.

His eyes make a slow, steady perusal of my body, taking the time to get their fill of me. They wander from my rounded breasts and flat stomach until they settle on what Blake undoubtedly wants most.

Blake runs his hand through my hair and my heart quickens at his touch. I want this so much that it physically hurts, but I would be lying if I said that I am not still frightened by what tonight means.

Does he want more? Am I ready for more if he does?

"Spread those legs wide for me." Blake's voice is laced with sweet, savage lust. It's controlled, but just barely. The undertone of desperation hidden there summons a sultry moan from my lips. Knowing that I have so much as an iota of an effect on him, sends a fresh wave of chills down my spine.

I do as I am told. Opening for him, letting my body fall back onto the cool floor, I spread my legs as wide apart as they can comfortably go, unashamed and completely at his mercy.

I don't know where what happens tonight will lead us. I don't know if we'll ever figure it out, but I do know one thing for certain—tonight, I am his and he, in all his dominant glory, is mine.

BLAKE

My dick throbs as Alyson spreads her long, toned legs apart for me, revealing her bare, glistening pussy. My mouth waters at the sight of her and I have to remind myself that I still have other plans for the evening.

"Close your eyes," I tell her and unlike a minute ago, this time there is no hesitation.

Reaching into the back pocket of my jeans, I pull out her red silk scarf, grateful that I have this opportunity to use it on her again. "I'm not going to fuck you, Alyson," I tell her as I slowly kneel near the top of her head.

I watch as her mouth opens as if to speak, but she apparently thinks better of it. She lets out a small whimper and I know that she is disappointed by what I just said.

Sliding my hand under the nape of her neck, I help her raise her head and I tie the scarf around it to cover her eyes. I groan at the sight before me. Alyson, blindfolded, her legs spread wide. The scent of her arousal and that intoxicating flowery perfume she's wearing fill my nostrils and stoke my desire.

So fucking perfect.

"I think we should play a little game." Still kneeling, I adjust my position, placing myself directly in front of her. My fingers graze the inside of her thigh and she moans in response. I tear my hand away from her silky skin, causing her to grumble yet again.

So impatient. I shake my head.

"Tell me, Alyson. Why did you storm out of my office the other day?"

I feel her body stiffen. Her breath catches in her throat and for a second I think she won't answer my question.

This won't do.

I repeat the question once again, becoming irritated that I am being forced to repeat myself. I suddenly plunge my finger into her pussy. "Don't make me ask again, Alyson! Remember what I told you? Lesson one is never to lie to your Dom."

She gasps in surprise and then moans in pleasure. "Oh, God. Blake, please," she's begging. I know exactly what she wants, but I still don't move my fingers.

"Alyson," I warn, and she quickly nods her head.

"I... I... I find it hard to believe that you will ever be satisfied with me, Sir," she confesses, her voice small and hesitant as she admits her truth.

I slowly begin to move my fingers in and out of her warm, sleek cunt. She moans her appreciation and grinds her hips as I continue to fuck her with my fingers.

How can she believe that I won't be satisfied with her? Doesn't she see how much she's affects me?

"And now? Do you feel that way now?" I ask, almost whispering. I don't want to hear her answer, but I know that this conversation is necessary. If she agrees to give us an honest chance, she'll have to know that she can tell me how she feels without fear of judgement.

She nods, sadly, biting her lower lip, and I feel a lump of emotion form in my throat.

How can she not see?

"Alyson," my voice is soft as I pull my fingers out of her and lean down so that I am now hovering over her. I kiss her throat, her shoulder, her neck. "You have no idea what you do to me." I kiss her ears, her cheek, and her forehead. "Since the moment I met you, you've been like a drug in my system that I never want to detox from."

Tears stream down the sides of her face, soaking the blindfold. I kiss each tear away. "But you want someone experienced, and you obviously don't do commitment..." she croaks, and my heart breaks at the pain that's evident in her voice.

I reach for the blindfold and pull it away, needing to see those gorgeous blue eyes. "I want you, Alyson. I've wanted you since the moment you sent me that first email. I want you and only you. I'm sorry that I haven't been clear in that regard, but I never planned for you. For us. Not after..."

"After what? Blake, please tell me. What caused you to become..." she stops short and looks me in the eye. "What happened to you?"

Looking down at her, I know that if this thing with Alyson is going to go anywhere I need to tell her everything, down to the last painful detail.

I pull away from her and stand up. She sits up and folds her legs up to her chest, wrapping her arms around them.

"I was engaged. Three years ago. We were going to have a baby. She was so stressed out, always working and never taking care of herself. I told her to rest. I told her that she had to think of the baby, but she insisted and I relented. I didn't stop her when she started catering more events than usual. I didn't question her when she came home late from an event, too exhausted to even hold up her head."

I'm now pacing back and forth, the images from three fucking years ago come rushing back as if they happened only yesterday, and although I want to scream, I press on. "I didn't want to argue with her. Didn't want to cause her more stress by insisting. By the time she was seven months along, we barely saw each other. I was working on the biggest case of my career and she was expanding her catering company."

I pause and take a deep breath. Outside of my therapist, I've never told anyone else about this. "One night, I came home late. I'd been working on that fucking case. The one case that was supposed to change our lives for the better." I shake my head, because that case did indeed change everything, but not in the way I thought it would. Not for the better.

"There was so much blood. So much. I didn't know what to do. She was crying hysterically and I couldn't get her to calm down. I got her to the hospital as quickly as I could."

Turning to face Alyson, I see the tears running down her face, her hand over her mouth.

"I lost them both that night. Pre-eclampsia, they told me," I whisper, turning away from her. "She and our child left me that night and I had no choice but to let them go."

ALYSON

"Oh, Blake. No, please don't think like that. How could you have known? How could either of you?" I scurry over to him, wrapping him in my arms.

I can't imagine how much he's suffered since his loss. My own loss comes to mind and I squeeze him even harder.

A few minutes pass before Blake breaks my hold on him and looks me in the eyes. "I've never told anyone about any of this shit. I'm glad that I told you," he says, before his lips comes crashing down on mine. His tongue pushes against my lips seeking entry and I give it to him, wanting him to take all the comfort he can from me.

He groans as the kiss ends and I can't help but ask the question I have been dying to have answered, "So... what happens now?"

As much as I need to hear his answer, my stomach churns at the possibility that I won't like what he has to say. He entered this lifestyle after losing the two people he loved. It's obviously been his escape—a way to take control of his life. Is he now ready to leave it behind, or at least find a happy medium? Do I want him to?

I want this life, with him. I can't imagine having any other version of Blake than the one I've been drawn to so deeply.

Blake smiles, and it's a genuine smile. He takes both of my hands into his and kisses each of my palms tenderly. "What happens now is that you're going to take that sexy ass of yours into your bedroom down the hall and get into the same position you were in that first night. Face down on the bed, on your stomach, your ass in the air."

"Blake," I scold, pulling my hands away from him. "You know what I mean. What happens between us? What are we doing?"

He grins, and shakes his head. It's then that what he said finally registers.

"My bedroom? What are you talking about?" I gasp.

"I don't know about you, but I plan on having you in a few minutes and I plan to repeat it every day that follows," he confirms with a knowing grin. "You're mine, Alyson. It's fast, I know, which is why you'll be staying here and not in my main condo, but I don't want us to be apart."

I'm speechless. Stunned into silence as my eyes wander the span of the room. "Blake, I… I can't live here. It's too much, too soon."

"Nonsense. You'll stay. Jaxon and the moving crew are already working on moving your things over. I want you here, Alyson," he says calmly, as if it's not a big deal.

But it is. It's a huge fucking deal.

"Okay…" I'm not comfortable with the idea, but I will do this for him. I understand why he needs me to be here. After what's told me, he has to be afraid of losing someone he cares about again.

"Wonderful. Now up to your room you go. Your first lesson will begin tonight."

He doesn't explain, and I don't question, "Yes, Sir."

EPILOGUE: ALYSON

The last few months have been amazing. Blake and I are practically living together, and while I was a bit anxious about it at first, it has gone smoothly.

Thank God.

The more time we spend together, the more normal he seems, and I can only assume it's because he's allowing more of his old self to surface.

I don't mind. I love the flowers he sends me for no reason at all, and the romantic dinners we share a few times a week. But, what I love most is that he still takes my breath away—each and every single night.

"Hands behind your back, Alyson." Blake kneels behind me on the bed as I bring my hands back, following his orders. I know what he's going to do. We've been training for this night for weeks, but I still feel a bit anxious.

"Just relax," he cajoles as he binds my hands together.

I take a calming breath, willing my body to unwind from its tense state. Clearing my mind, I tell myself that I trust Blake and that he will guide me through this.

Blake begins by massaging my shoulders, his hands nicely oiled. I moan at his caress, loving the feel of his strong hands on my body. Those hands. They've brought me nothing but pleasure in the last few months and I feel secure in the knowledge that I am in good hands with Blake.

Slowly he moves his hands from my shoulders to my back, kneading in a circular motion and taking away all my apprehension. He manipulates my body expertly, and I fall into a blissful state of peace as his hands descend down my body.

"You're so beautiful," he whispers, when he reaches my bottom, his hands, giving my cheeks the same loving treatment he's given my tense shoulders.

I sigh, "Thank you, Sir."

The feel of more oil trailing down my back eases me, and even though I know what's coming, I don't tense up.

I want this. With him. Only with him.

BLAKE

I am in complete awe of this woman. She's given me so much in the short time we've been together and tonight, she freely gives me the only part of her I've left untouched.

What have I done to deserve her?

Slowly, I let my fingers circle her forbidden channel. Alyson swoons, but settles down as I continue to massage her rear opening. She's been wearing the plugs I purchased for her, so I know that she won't experience too much pain.

But my crafty little woman loves the pain I give her.

I adjust myself so that my cock is now positioned at the entrance to her pussy, and I push forward as I also insert just one finger inside her ass. She moans, encouraging me to continue and I do.

Moving my finger in and out of her ass, in the same rhythm as I'm moving my cock, she shudders with pleasure and I insert another finger alongside the first, testing her channel before I take her where she needs to go. Increasing my speed, she cries out, her slickened pussy tightly clamping down my cock, and I know that she is close.

Snaking my free hand around her waist, I find her swollen clit and apply just enough pressure to tip her over the edge as I rock into her, her hips pushing back in time to meet me.

"Fuck. Oh, Blake," she cries, just as she falls over the edge into her orgasm, but I am far from finished.

Removing my fingers from her rear, I quickly grab onto her ponytail and give it a quick tug, and she groans at the pain. Before she comes down from her high, in one swift motion, I take her in the ass and she gasps in surprise.

"Oh, fuck. Alyson, you feel so fucking amazing," I groan, loving the feel of her tight ass around my cock. I still my body, giving her ass a chance to adjust to its sudden impalement. She'll need to be completely comfortable and relaxed if this experience is going to be pleasurable for her, and that's what I want it to be.

"Baby, you take over for a while. I'm far too tempted to fuck you hard and long when you feel so damn good around me," I tell her.

She giggles, but makes no move to take the reins, "Sir, you may take me any way you like. My body is yours to do with as you wish."

A guttural growl tears out of me at the sound of her submission and it's all the encouragement I need.

So fucking perfect.

God, I love her.

THE END!

www.ingramcontent.com/pod-product-compliance
Lightning Source LLC
Chambersburg PA
CBHW061143170626
46809CB00003B/969